DEATH & DRAGON

The Channeler Trilogy Book Three

J. Steven Lamperti

ISBN-13 : 978-1734597493

Lamprey Publishing
LampreyPublishing@gmail.com

Cover titles and frame by James, GoOnWrite.com

Map by Johnny Quan

Printed in the United States of America

The Channeler Trilogy

Moon & Shadow

Sun & Dream

Death & Dragon

The Tales of Liamec

The Wolf's Tooth

By the Sea

Twilight's Fall

The Channeler Trilogy

Sunshine over Hero

The Pirates of Meara

Endymion and the Fae

Dedicated to Sebastian,
who was the first,
and started it all for me.

AUTHOR'S NOTE

Death & Dragon is the concluding volume of the Channeler Trilogy, following *Moon & Shadow* and *Sun & Dream*. It is written with the expectation that the previous two books have already been read.

This book is not intended to stand alone. Its meaning, its choices, and its ending are built on the story that comes before it. Readers who have followed Anise's journey from the beginning will find that this final volume brings that story to its intended close.

A brief recap follows for orientation. It is not meant to replace reading the earlier books, but to remind you how the path to this ending was laid.

RECAP

Anise is a young channeler in training. Channeling is a form of magic where a mage conjures a spirit or daemon in their dreams and gets the being to help with a problem in the waking world.

Anise and her Uncle Sebastian traveled across the land of Liamec several years ago so she could begin studying the ways of magic at the Academy, the magical school of the land. Sebastian's old adversary, Lorenzo, had become a master at the Academy. Sebastian was convinced that Lorenzo had reformed from his earlier dangerous ways. Lorenzo is now the channeling department's headmaster and welcomes Anise to the Academy.

Anise learns and studies magic at the Academy, becoming increasingly more in control of her abilities. Several years of study lead her to a feeling of confidence and strength. However, right after graduation, her trust is shattered. Master Lorenzo uses his powers to walk into Anise's dreams and talk to her in the dream realm. After trying to explain himself, Lorenzo pushes Anise out of her circle of light. The circle of light is that safe zone channelers need to stay within to remain sane and protected from the realm of Dream.

Anise falls into the darkness and unknown dangers of the dream realm.

PROLOGUE

She was falling, falling through a dream. Anise still felt the pressure on her back where master Lorenzo had shoved her. She was confused. *Why had he pushed her?* Then she felt hurt. *I trusted him.* Then she felt anger. *Never again. From now on, people will have to earn my trust.*

She wasn't falling fast. It was somewhere between a float and a fall. She could look around her as she dropped. *Am I falling asleep or falling awake?* She wondered.

She was falling through some sort of vertical tunnel. Rough earthen walls surrounded her on all sides. It wasn't uniform, though; side channels and chambers opened up around her. Some of them might lead outside the tunnel.

Scenes floated by in the side chambers. An armored figure led a line of red-clad women through exercise drills. A dragon flew above an inky, black night sky. *Was that a person riding on the dragon's back?* A blacksmith pounded on his anvil. An open green field of grass surrounded a bright red barn. It was too much to take in.

Anise wasn't sure how long she'd been falling. She wasn't sure if she'd been falling for a minute, an hour, or a day. As sometimes happens in a dream, her sense of time abandoned her.

Another thing. *Had she been pushed, or had she fallen off a horse or some other animal she had been riding?* Both felt right. Anise was confused.

She didn't have time to think about it. A surface was coming up below. Anise tried to twist and turn so that she could land on her feet.

DREAM

1

I t was a small village of perhaps fifteen to twenty houses. Nestled among the trees of the green forest, under the clear blue sky, you might have thought it a romantic, picturesque sight. Until that is, you saw the villagers being led, manacled in chains, in a column into the central town square.

Groups of armed men dressed in chain mail were escorting the line of bound people. Some of the villagers in the column were weeping, some complained, and others just sullenly and grimly accepted their lot.

In addition to those escorting the villagers, other armed men moved about in the village. All were dressed in purple tabards over their chain mail. The bright purple color of the tabard was broken by a black silhouette of a coiled serpent about to strike.

The men who weren't escorting the column were ducking into houses, overturning haystacks, and breaking open barrels. Looking to see if they had missed any villagers.

It took a moment for the men in their purple to notice the lone figure standing at the forest's edge. The sunlight shone down on the figure, dressed head to toe in black. The sunlight shone down, but somehow, it failed to illuminate the shape. The black clothing, of some indeterminate material, not linen, metal, leather, but something other, absorbed the light. It sucked the light rays into it, not reflecting, not brightening, and not allowing any of it to escape.

It took a moment for the men in purple to notice the figure, but once they noticed, it didn't take them long to react. The first one to see the shape let loose with a cry, almost like a scream. Then, as if embarrassed at his initial reaction, he stopped what he was doing, pointed at the figure, and bellowed, "There!"

Another of the men, startled, gawked at the figure and called out loudly, "It's Death's Daughter; sound the signal!"

The figure reacted for the first time. It moved, taking a step forward into the light. The sunbeams, who had been so reluctant to illuminate the shape, relented a little. The black silhouette of the figure resolved itself into a woman's form. A woman stood on the clearing's edge, clad in tight, inky material that flowed over her. Her head was enclosed in a black helmet. Dark like her clothing, the helmet was made of similar material. It showed a white outline of a skull embossed into the front.

One of the men pulled out a horn and blew a shrill blast. The rest stopped and stood expectantly as if waiting for something.

Armed guards started pouring out of the houses. It was evident that the earlier action had been a bit of an act, as, with all these armed men inside the buildings, the searching hadn't been necessary. Many of the men were bowmen. The bowmen formed up into ranks and readied their weapons.

The woman hardly seemed to notice the archers preparing to fire. There was a wisp of smoke curling around her left shoulder. At times the smoky tendrils looked like they formed a shape.

The archery captain stepped forward. "Nock!" he called out, followed quickly by "Mark!" and then, "Draw!" The archers pulled back on their bowstrings. The woman hardly moved.

"Loose!" called out the captain. A volley of arrows arched through the air toward the dark figure at the edge of the clearing.

2

The woman responded to the flight of arrows. Lifting her right arm, she splayed the fingers of her hand out toward the sky. The quantity of smoke on her shoulder solidified into some sort of creature, perhaps the size of a large cat, before turning back into vapor. A tendril of the smoke crept out from the mass and wound around the woman's neck.

A sheet of flame surged forth from her fingertips. Several archers recoiled from the heat, even standing on the other side of the open space. The fire rose, crackling into the sky. The arrows weren't just singed and seared but were also pushed back, tumbling from the sky as if the flames were more solid than simply heat and fire.

As the flames burst among the arrows and they burned, the air grew chill. Some of the archers shivered. Frost started forming on the leaves of the trees edging the clearing. The chill of death was in the air. Persephone, mother winter, was kissing Hades, father death, in that green space.

One archer crossed himself and cried out, "Spawn of Thanatos!" He broke from the end of the line and ran for the woods. The others looked after him like they wished they could do the same.

As the archery captain began readying his men for another volley, soldiers armed with weapons other than bows formed into a line. Their captain drew his sword, raised it above his head, and called out, "Charge!" The row of men, clad in their chain mail and purple tabards and armed with shields and swords, began racing across the clearing.

The woman readied a short spear she had strapped to her back. The weapon lengthened as she drew it from a sheath across her shoulder until it was a bit longer than half her height. Holding the spear in her right hand, she reached out with her left hand, splayed the fingers on her hand again, and raised it, palm upward towards the sky.

Stones burst forth from the ground, shooting into the air with great force. The men standing above where the rocks sprang from were brushed aside like flies. The rest, with some hesitation, kept charging forward.

The archery captain recited his litany of "Nock! Mark!" and then "Loose!" again. Another rain of arrows came arching through the sky.

The woman crouched, lifting her left arm above her head to guard herself. A black shield appeared on the raised arm as the arrows pelted down. Black, except for the golden outline of an owl's face embossed on the surface. The arrows splintered on the shield or were knocked aside.

The woman rose, facing the men almost upon her, her spear in her right hand. The shield vanished from her left arm. In a voice hardly recognizable as human, amplified by something, perhaps the helmet, she said, "You sold your souls for profit, safety, and money. I hope the judges of the underworld will have mercy on you when you reach the other side because I will not." With a quick motion, almost too quick, she hurled the spear. It flew across the distance and struck the captain of the charging soldiers square in the chest. Somehow it pierced through him, kept on moving, and inscribed a great arc through the sky above the clearing until it returned with a small clank into her gloved hand.

The troop captain crumpled to the green grass, surprised to find himself lifeless. The men, clad in their purple, almost as one, broke and fled the clearing. Many dropped their shields and weapons on the grass as they ran.

3

Anise twisted and just managed to get her feet under her as she landed on a narrow path's rough dirt and stones. She caught her balance. The trail wound its way through a valley between some hills. The trees lining both sides of the track looked stunted, scraggly, and barren. Everything was dry and brown. A chill, stale breeze blew by her.

Anise started walking. A dreamy confusion overtook her. She lost track of whether she had just gotten here or if she had been walking for a long while. The trail led onward through the dry forest toward a mountain pass in the distance. A shudder of panic went through her. Anise didn't remember when she had started walking; she didn't remember where she was going.

She swallowed. Her throat felt dry, parched. The dry air felt hostile, unwelcoming, inhospitable to life. She looked again at the brown hills, the barren trees, and the mountains in the distance. Everything looked dry. The sky loomed gray overhead, cloudless but still not clear.

Anise felt a little cold; it wasn't just the cool, dry air. She felt the chill of loneliness and uncertainty. She pulled the sides of her cloak tighter around her. It was the warm red cloak Maeve had given her when it got frosty last winter. Anise didn't remember putting it on.

Anise frowned. *What did she remember?* She didn't know where she was or why she was here. The last thing she remembered was her graduation ceremony and the celebration with her friends afterward. After four years of study at the academy, she had graduated. Her friends had been discussing what they would do next. What she had been looking forward to most was traveling home and seeing her

Aunts Rose and Isabel and her Uncle Sebastian.

She almost teared up when she thought about Aunt Rose. Rose had been her only living blood relative since the death of her parents. Sebastian and Isabel were like family, but Rose was family. Anise had already been missing Rose even before whatever was happening to her now had happened.

Suddenly she was overcome with relief; this was just a dream. She was still asleep. She was sleeping in, in the morning. Soon she would wake up in the way-house, where she had been living for the last years while going to school.

Gradually the relief turned back to unease. This wasn't just a dream; it was a dream of power, a channeling dream. It was a channeling dream, and Anise couldn't feel her circle of safety, her circle of light. *What would master Callum say?* She thought.

The memory came unbidden of a section in the book she had read for master Huginn in clairvoyance class. The *Archipelago of Dream* had a part where the unnamed writer described a place called the Dry Lands. The land between Death and Dream, he'd called it. The book had been long on ornate description and philosophy but short on down-to-earth details. Her recollection was that he had only been able to leave the Dry Lands with the help of his dragon guide. In fact, most things the writer had escaped or survived had been through the agency of his escort.

Anise looked around her. *Where was her dragon guide?*

Anise started. There was a man next to her, walking beside her. Had he been there the whole time? She looked more carefully. It was master Lorenzo. "Master Lorenzo," said Anise. "How are you here? Where are we?" She frowned. "Wait," she said, "you pushed me! Why did you push me?"

4

Anise turned and glared at master Lorenzo, waiting for a response. She shook her head in surprise. It wasn't master Lorenzo. How had she ever thought it was? It was Uncle Sebastian. Anise opened her mouth, excited, and began rattling out some words for her beloved uncle.

"Uncle Sebastian," she said, "I'm so glad to see you. I don't know where I am. It's so dry here." Her uncle's steady, calm presence encouraged her, and she continued. "I'm so sorry about Twilight. I wish I could have protected him. He was so young."

"Don't worry about your young charge, Anise," said the figure beside her. "His time is not over, and his story is just beginning. It'll turn out to be quite a story."

Anise turned to look. The voice had calm, reassuring tones, like her uncle, but it didn't sound like him. Anyway, what did it mean about Twilight's story not being over?

It wasn't Uncle Sebastian, after all. The man walking beside her was a tall, pale man dressed in flowing black robes. A group of tiny, winged men and women flapped around him like a flock of birds. The wings on these little people looked bat-like. The man himself looked bemused.

Distractedly he turned to Anise and said, "You know, Anise, your soul, life, and sanity should be forfeit to me, lord Morpheus." The bemused look changed to a slightly more attentive smile with a smooth transition. "But, someone higher up wants you alive and relatively sane." He laughed, "We all have higher powers to whom we have to attend." Anise remembered that Lord Morpheus was the king and lord of the realm of dream. The little creatures fluttering around him must be the Oneiroi.

A little man no taller than a mouse, one of the tiny

people, flitted over to Anise. Its little bat wings blew the dusty air into her face. She flinched a little as it flew toward her.

The little creature silently landed on Anise's shoulder, then stretched and morphed into something else. Its wings changed shape; it grew. Anise recoiled but was too scared to try to brush it off. As the creature changed shape, it began turning into something more familiar. After a moment, it was Iggy riding on her shoulder.

"Iggy," called out Anise happily. Anything familiar was comfort. The fire imp who had started as a reading aid in the Academy library and escaped through Anise's channeling met her gaze with his cat-like eyes. He settled in. His tail crept around Anise's neck lovingly. He touched her forehead lightly with one of his talons. "Burn," he said reassuringly.

Morpheus watched this with patience and calm that felt somewhat abstract. "Do you have any questions for me?" he said. "Time and night are wasting."

Anise turned her attention back to the pale man. "You said someone wants me safe? Who? Is it Lord Helios?"

Lord Morpheus shifted back to his inattentive smile. Anise felt she preferred the calm. "I didn't exactly say safe," he said. "The sun's rays do not reach into the Dry Lands, the realm of Dream, or the underworld, so, no, not the god of the sun."

The lord got a slightly more attentive look on his face. "I must be off. I don't have time to spend with every lost soul with a bad dream." He lifted his arms. The little bat-winged men and women flew up into the sky. The black robes fluttered and wavered, and then there was nothing but a cloud of little winged men and women flitting off in a flock into the dry breeze.

5

Iggy stayed, reassuringly, on Anise's shoulder. He uncoiled the end of his tail from her neck and pointed it along the path. "Burn," he said persuasively. With nowhere else to go, and nothing else to do, Anise resumed her walk up the trail toward the distant, dry mountain pass.

With Iggy on her shoulder, Anise moved forward with renewed confidence, though she still had no idea where she was going. Looking ahead up the path toward the mountains in the distance, she had the feeling that everywhere in this dry, forsaken land would be the same. Still, a trail had to go somewhere, and she couldn't help but think that anywhere would be better than whatever or wherever here was.

Anise thought about trying to wake up. She knew how to wake herself from a channeling dream. She always had. Though, until her channeling classes at the Academy, she hadn't known why or what she knew.

What you did was you thought of your circle of light, the safe space within your dream, as a loop that you could jump through or move through. It wasn't a physical thing, more of a mental exercise. Without her circle, and the absence was almost painful, Anise had no idea what to do.

She felt a momentary sensation, almost as if a door was opening. A ghostly figure appeared in front of her, beside the track. Iggy looked up expectantly, "Burn?" he said.

The figure stepped forward. Shadowy and transparent, it gestured to Anise urgently.

"Master Callum?" she asked.

It was the master. At least it looked like him. Like he looked in Dream. Handsome and young, his semi-transparent brown hair waving in the dry wind. She remembered how her channeling master's face looked in the waking world, with the massive scarring from a childhood injury.

"Anise," he said, "You have to come with me. You have to wake up."

"You're just another dream," said Anise. She felt angry. As if someone was playing a trick on her.

"No," said the master sadly, "I'm really here. You have to wake up, Anise."

He did something then. He grabbed her somehow. Not physically, but with his will, with his spirit. Anise had the feeling that he was trying to pull her through his circle of light. It hurt. It felt wrong. Somehow she knew that he was trying to help, that he thought he might be able to wake her this way. Somehow she also knew that it wouldn't work. It would kill her or rend her soul.

Iggy opened his mouth and blew a blast of fire at the ghostly master. The flames passed through the figure without effect.

"Master Callum," she cried, "No, it won't work." She fought back. She resisted.

Something ripped. Something tore. Anise saw master Callum's figure recede toward his vanishing circle of light. At the same time, the brown hills, the gray sky, and the dirt trail shredded apart into a haze of dust, and she was falling again.

6

Anise shifted her weight. She felt off-kilter, as if she had just landed after a fall. She adjusted her balance and felt more stable. She looked around. The sky felt familiar, gray and brooding, dry like an old bone, but unexpressive.

Nothing else did, however. *Where was she?* She was standing at the top of a hill. A green grassy slope stretched before her down the hill toward a split rail fence at the bottom. Both sides of the grassy slope were lined with trees. The brilliant green grass and the trees were so lush and inviting that they felt surreal. When she took in the sky and its expanse of dry gray, her throat felt parched as if she hadn't had a drop in a week. When she gazed at the green grass and the leaves of the trees, she felt the opposite. It felt so lush, fertile, and pregnant with life that she wanted to spend time rolling in it.

Beyond the fence was a further field of rich green grass, and beyond that was a large building that she assumed must be a barn from its appearance. It was bigger than her uncle's barn. Much bigger. It was also bright red. The fiery bright red color made any red dye or paint she had ever seen feel pale. The red hue of the cloak Maeve had given her was nothing to that color. Next to the barn was a cylindrical tower with a domed roof. It also was painted the same bright red.

Between the fence and the barn was a broad field. There was a herd of something roaming the grass. From her height, she couldn't make out what kind of animals they were, but she could recognize the patterns of herding and the motions of a herd. She felt she could almost make out the herder, though something looked a little peculiar about that also.

Anise felt a weight on her left shoulder. She looked and saw Iggy looking back at her implacably. The tip of his tail unwound itself from her neck and pointed down the hill. "Burn," said Iggy conversationally. As she met his gaze, the fire imp faded from a solid creature resting on her shoulder into a nebulous column of smoke. There was still a wisp of sooty vapor pointing toward the barn.

"Iggy?" said Anise.

"Burn," a calm voice whispered in her ear.

Anise started down the hill toward the fence, as she had nothing better to do.

7

Halfway down the hill, Anise saw something on the grassy slope ahead of her. As she approached the fence and beyond it, the field and barn, a sense of dread fell upon her. She pulled the hood of her cloak up over her head. It made her feel a little safer. Whatever this shape was, investigating it would delay her reaching the pasture, which was welcome.

It was a sundial. A few years ago, Brone, the town scribe of Hero, had gotten hold of a translated Persian scroll that detailed this marvelous time engine. He had persuaded Victor Potter, the tombstone maker, to make him one. The mayor had initially been quite impressed. He had set up a place on the edge of the cobbled town square for the sundial. He was sure that this unique device would encourage the tourist trade he knew was soon and inevitably coming to Hero.

When this failed to happen, and when the villagers commented that they knew perfectly well what time it was by looking at the sun's position in the sky, he became disillusioned with the technology.

This sundial looked similar to the one that still graced the town square of Hero. Built of stone, it had a column, which was topped with a circular platform marked with lines and words. It was crowned by a triangular wedge meant to catch the sun's rays and cast a shadow on the lines below. It stood on a level place in the grass of the slope. The dazzling green continued above and below it.

Anise realized two things as she looked more closely at the device. The first was that she had seen no trace of the sun on her descent down the hill. The gray sky was uniform, cloudless and sunless. She hesitated; hadn't someone told her that the sun didn't shine here?

The other thing was that the sundial's circular piece was draped or stretched over the top of the stone column like a wad of pastry dough. It reminded Anise of her aunt kneading bread in her bakery. The triangular stone wedge still stood on top, but the stone circle flowed and drooped down the sides of the column.

Anise shivered. The sheer pointlessness of this bothered her.

Perhaps sensing her distress, Iggy stroked her shoulder with the tip of his tail.

"Burn," he said convincingly.

8

Anise drew nearer to the fence. The herd was moving her way. She was interested to see what manner of animals they were. Sebastian kept cows, but other farmers in Hero raised pigs, sheep, and goats. There were, of course, also geese and chickens, though you wouldn't keep them in a field such as this. She marveled again at the size and bright color of the barn. It must be a wealthy farm she was approaching.

She heard the crack of a distant whip, and the herd wheeled in her direction. A thin cloud of dust was in the air around the animals, obscuring her view. The pasture grass inside the fence was less lush than the hillside. Patches of dirt and dust showed through between the stretches of green. The lead animals pulled toward her, breaking through the dust.

Anise gasped. The herd wasn't animals at all; it was people. The herd leaders raced toward her, veering off to one side at the last minute to avoid the fence. They were men and women in various stages of dress and of different ages.

A middle-aged woman charged by Anise bellowing. She wore what might once have been an elegant dress, but it was torn and ragged. Her face was a mask of non-focused rage. Following her was a young man. He looked panicked but, at the same time, focused, like there was someplace he needed to be so urgently that he wouldn't let anything stand in his way. He was bare-chested and had on ratty linen britches. Next was an older man, then a young girl. Each was as focused as the last.

The herd thundered by. Anise tried to get the attention of some of the runners, but they ignored her. Each was absolutely fixated on following the person in front of them.

She was standing just on the other side of the fence. As the last of the herd rumbled by, the herder came into view. Curious at first who could be herding such a mob, Anise regretted her curiosity when the herder turned to look at her.

It was a woman. Or was it? Naked from the waist up, the herder had the body of a young woman. Still, Anise had never seen a young woman with either a pair of wings that should be on a giant eagle or the head of a wrinkled crone.

Flying low so that the tips of her eagle wings just brushed the ground, the herder cracked a leather whip at her charges whenever one strayed from the herd. She wore black leather pants and boots. Her gray hair was cut short, and wrinkles and other age marks painted her face.

The winged woman met Anise's gaze as she flew by the fence. Anise had never seen such a look of anger. The raw scorn coming from the woman made Anise feel guilty about things she hadn't even done yet.

The whip arm drew back. Anise braced for the blow. Just then, one of the herd bellowed and broke from the pack. A boy. He couldn't have been more than fifteen. He split from the herd and started away from the fence, in the direction of the barn.

The herder woman halted her whip swing, wheeled her flight off toward the boy's path, and moved away from the fence.

"That was a close one, wasn't it?" said a voice.

9

Anise looked to her right as the herd thundered off toward her left on the other side of the fence. A young woman walked toward her, her mouth stretched wide in a big toothy grin. She wore cloth britches with a partial leather covering over them. The leather was more on the inside of her legs than the outside. *Maybe for riding?* Thought Anise. She had on a loose gray top and a broad-rimmed hat. Her smile was so infectious that Anise immediately felt an affinity for her.

"Anise," she said. "Welcome to the farm. Let me help you over the fence." She stepped forward, put her foot on the first rail, and held out her hand.

Anise hesitated. She heard a low hiss near her ear from Iggy.

"How come everyone knows my name?" she complained. "I don't know yours."

"We don't get many visitors," said the young woman cheerfully, "Especially not ones that drop in the way you did."

Iggy turned to smoke again. The sounds in Anise's ear were like a hissing, sizzling campfire as it's being put out. Anise moved forward and climbed over the fence, taking the young woman's hand as she reached the top. Her grip felt firm and warm.

"Let's go up to the barn for a bite," the woman said when Anise's feet were on the ground on the other side of the fence. "Some breakfast?"

Anise thought about it. "What time is it?" she said. "Is it breakfast time?"

The woman laughed. Her smile broadened as she laughed. "Does it matter?" she asked. "It's always time to break one's fast for someone, somewhere."

They started walking toward the red barn. The shorter grass and dusty dirt felt reassuring under Anise's feet. A momentary breeze blew, and she pulled the sides of her cloak a little tighter against the chill.

"So, who are you?" said Anise, "What's your name?"

"Lyssa," said the woman. Her smile grew even broader. Anise wasn't sure the smile was so charming anymore. There were a few too many teeth showing. She thought about the name. It was familiar. She should remember something about it, but at the moment, she didn't.

The group of people running along the fence turned toward them. Anise noticed two other herds in the field. They had been too distant to be seen from above, but they were coming closer now. Each of the others was being driven by a woman like the first. They looked enough alike to be sisters.

"Should we get out of the way?" said Anise. "They're coming this way."

"It's alright," said Lyssa. "It's not a problem."

The herds closed in on them. The herders stopped their flocks just short of running over Anise and Lyssa. Soon they were enclosed in a circle of the herded people. Anise tried to meet the gaze of one young woman wearing the tatters of a yellow smock. All she saw was a disturbing, unfocused stare.

Iggy was hissing like a teakettle about to burst. Anise thought about preparing her elemental abilities to defend herself, but she was in Dream. There was no connection with the elemental forces in the dream realm.

Lyssa turned to Anise. Her smile broadened even more. It was wider than should have been feasible. Sharp teeth were showing at the corners of her mouth. Anise thought she saw flecks of foam there as well.

Anise shied back. "Why are your teeth so sharp?" she whispered.

"The better to eat you with, my dear," said Lyssa. She moved toward Anise. Her mouth opened wider than humanly possible. A row of razor-sharp teeth, dripping with foam, gleamed pearly white.

10

Iggy tensed on Anise's shoulder. It was surprising that she could even tell because he was still just a curling wisp of smoke, but something about the curl seemed tense, and she heard a low growl in her ear. The three herders readied their whips, and Lyssa moved toward her.

A sound arose at the back of the milling crowd of humans. The herd stirred and grew disquieted. This clearly wasn't something Lyssa was expecting. She stopped her advance toward Anise to look.

Cries of "Pardon me," "excuse me," and "sorry" were heard as a man made his way through the crowd. The herd gave way to him surprisingly freely. Even one of the herders stepped out of his way as he emerged from the mob.

The smile that had never left Lyssa's face, even when that face hadn't looked human, left it now.

"Koalemos," she said. "What is it? It's not a good time. I'm in the middle of something."

Anise scanned the man. He was big. Dressed in a dark blue tunic and brown britches, he was taller than many in the mob he had made his way through. A little bit of a belly pushed out the blue fabric of his tunic. He had a smile on his face. Though she had begun to doubt her ability to judge, Anise thought it was a more genuine smile than Lyssa's. He didn't seem to have a weapon on him.

"So sorry, Lyssa," said the big man. He was panting a bit as if the exertion of pushing his way through the herd had tired him. "I don't mean to interrupt; it's just that my cousin asked me to do him a favor."

Lyssa looked annoyed. "Your cousin," she said, "Which cousin? You have so many. I'm one of your cousins."

Koalemos just stared at her. His face seemed to imply

that she should know the answer to her question.

"Oh," Lyssa said.

Anise wasn't sure what to do. Should she be irritated or relieved that they were just ignoring her?

"She is not yours," the big man said. "Our cousin just wanted you to know that she is under his protection."

Anise stamped her foot. "Why does everybody keep talking about whose I am. I'm not any of yours. I'm not yours," looking at Lyssa, "I'm not his," with a wave in a direction that might have been toward Morpheus if she had any idea where he was. "I'm not your cousin's," glancing at Koalemos. "I'm my own. You all may be gods, or whatever you are, but that still doesn't mean you own me."

Koalemos sadly met Anise's eyes. "That's one of those things we keep telling ourselves, isn't it?" he said. Lyssa looked angry. The smile that had faded from her face a while ago didn't look like it was coming back soon. The three furious herder sisters were standing by for a cue from her. The human herds were waiting for a whip to crack.

Koalemos reached out and took Anise's hand. "My lady," he said, "If I may, I would like to take you from this place. It's not a good place for the likes of you."

Anise looked down at her hand lying in Koalemos's larger, slightly beefy one. "Can I trust you?"

"Well," said Koalemos, "Trust." He hesitated. "That's a difficult thing to come by." He indicated the human herds, the three herders, and Lyssa with his eyes and a head motion. "I would like to think that you can trust me more than you can trust them."

Koalemos smiled. "Let's take a little leap of faith together." He made a motion as if preparing to hop up into the air.

Anise followed, and the two of them, hand in hand, made a slight jump up and down on the dusty ground.

Lyssa howled. The sky, ground, and everything else fractured into brown dust. The last thing Anise saw was Lyssa's mouth opening again, showing her gleaming foam splattered teeth.

The world splintered into fragments, and Anise was falling again.

KOALEMOS

1

The landing was a little smoother this time. Koalemos held her hand, which made the twisting turn to get her feet beneath her a little easier. She still staggered a bit on the impact, however. Anise tried to look around herself. It was hard, as there wasn't anything to focus on. She was surrounded by a borderless expanse of white. Iggy made a puzzled fizzling sound in her ear. Koalemos stood next to her.

"Welcome to my home. My safe place," he said.

"There's nothing here," said Anise.

"I haven't had time to decorate," said Koalemos. He sounded a little sad.

"Shouldn't there at least be some walls or something?" said Anise.

"Oh," said Koalemos, "That's clever. Why didn't I think of that." He made a gesture with his hands, both palms facing outward. Stone walls appeared around them, a stone floor below and a recessed ceiling above. It made Anise think of a monk's cell in a monastery. There were no openings in the uniform surfaces of paved stone.

"It's a little claustrophobic," said Anise.

"Right," said Koalemos. He made little twisting gestures with his fingers. Two windows and a wooden door appeared in the walls. The windows looked out onto the same white expanse as before.

"So," said Anise, "it's time for some answers," she gestured behind herself as if that was the direction where Lyssa was, "Who was that? And, who are you?"

Koalemos looked flustered. "I'm Koalemos," he said, "but please call me Cole. Not everyone does, but I'd like it if they did." He hesitated. "I guess I'm in charge of those people who know less about the world than they should or than the world knows about them." He hesitated again. "Some of my relatives think that I am one of those."

"And," said Anise, "who was that?" She pointed again.

"Lyssa?" said Cole, "She's my cousin. She's in charge of those people who know too much about the world and for whom the world is too much." He looked down at the stone floor. "She doesn't treat them very well." He glanced up at Anise. "She's usually the one who gets the ones who come here the way you did."

"All right," said Anise slowly. "And who did you say it was who asked you to help me?"

Cole looked a little nervous. "I'd rather not say," he said.

2

Anise looked out the window at the borderless white expanse. She had suggested some furniture to Cole and was sitting comfortably in a high wooden rocking chair. It had a pleasantly soft embroidered cushion on it. It was embroidered with the words, "Home, sweet home." She rocked gently back and forth.

"Some flowers might look nice out there," she said. Instantly a row of bright purple blooms appeared, bordering one edge of the expanse. "They shouldn't all look exactly the same," she continued.

"Sorry," said Cole. He sounded embarrassed. He waved his hand, and the heights of some of the flowers varied a little bit. Anise decided to let it go.

"Can you help me get out of here?" she asked. "Can you help me leave the world of dream?"

"I'm sorry, Anise," said Cole. "There are rules."

"Rules?" said Anise. "Whose rules! What rules?"

"Sorry," said Cole. "That's one of the rules. I can't tell you."

Anise sighed. "Well, maybe some of Aunt Rose's raisin pastries, then," she said.

A table appeared between her and Cole, loaded down with baked goods. Anise smelled the delicious odor of her aunt's work.

Cole picked up one of the raisin pastries and took a bite. His face lit up in pleasure.

"Theesh aar guud," he said through a mouthful of cake and raisins.

Anise picked one up and took a bite herself.

Cole looked sadly down at the ground. There was a woolen carpet covering the cold stone floor. "I'm sorry, Anise, it's time we said goodbye."

"Said goodbye?" said Anise, "Where are you going?"

"I'm not going anywhere," said Cole, "you are."

"I have nowhere to go," said Anise sadly.

"Even so, you still have a long journey in front of you," said Cole. He waved his hand. The chair, stone walls, raisin pastries, even Cole himself started dissolving, and Anise was falling again.

Anise landed on her rear on a dirt trail. "Ow," she said bitterly. Fortunately, she wasn't falling fast enough to hurt herself. She looked up. Both sides of the path were lined with scraggly dry leafless trees. Brown hills stood beyond them.

"Burn," said Iggy sympathetically.

Anise picked herself up, brushed off the dust, and tried to figure out where she was. *Dream, of course, but which part of Dream?*

The brown hills, gray sky, and dry air made her remember the Dry Lands from the book *The Archipelago of Dream*. Between Death and Dream, the author had said.

Anise tried to remember what else he had said about the Dry Lands in the book. He had described the place as a crossroads, where he stopped between visits to other parts of Dream and other places. She hadn't really been paying too much attention, as she had thought the book the ramblings of a madman. She regretted that now.

There was only one trail. Anise started walking forward. The brown hills on both sides were featureless. There was a mountain in the distance in front of her, and somehow the air looked clearer there. *Is that a spot of green on the mountainside?* She thought. Anything would be better than the unrelenting dryness and brownness of the trees lining the trail.

Iggy flapped above her. Around a turn in the trail, they came to a fork. Anise gazed at the fire imp. "Burn," said Iggy doubtfully. He seemed like he shrugged his shoulders, though he had such a thick neck that the motion was almost imperceptible.

Anise inspected the trails. The left branch might be

headed more toward the distant mountain. She went that way.

There was no way to judge time with no sun in the sky and the uniform light. The mountain didn't seem to get any closer.

"Iggy," said Anise, "You don't remember any of the chapters from that book, do you?"

"Burn," said Iggy with a firm shake of his head.

4

Anise twisted her falling body to try to land smoothly on the rough warm stone floor beneath her. She caught her balance. It was starting to feel normal to rise into consciousness as if she had just recovered from a fall. In front of her was an archway. A flow of warm air blew through the opening. The stones that made up the arch were old, ancient. They were covered with lingering traces of soot. They'd been burned or exposed to fire at some point. Behind her ..., but she couldn't look behind herself for some reason. She didn't want to; she didn't need to; she couldn't.

Iggy chirped excitedly on Anise's shoulder. It was a sound she'd never heard him make before. It was almost as if he felt some welcoming presence or familiarity with where they were. She stepped forward through the archway.

The warm air flowed past her as she moved down the stone passage. It felt more like a tunnel than a corridor. The walls were natural rock, though there were signs that they had been widened. The sooty look continued. The air smelled a little smoky as well. It smelled a little like the smell you got when you put a piece of metal into a campfire. The tunnel was broad and high.

As Anise moved down the warm tunnel, a sound that she had heard with the tail end of her attention started getting louder and louder. It was a metallic rhythmic ringing sound. She turned a corner in the tunnel, the sound grew loud enough to become unpleasant, and she recognized it. It was the rhythm of a blacksmith's hammer. A little further, the corridor opened out into a large rocky chamber, and she saw the smith.

His forge was against the far wall, the massive anvil beside it. Waves of heat surged into the room from the open flames of the forge. There was a rough wooden workspace to one side covered with iron tools. A trough of water stood on the other side.

The smith himself had his back to her. His arm was lifted, holding a hammer whose head had to be as big as Anise's, if not larger. The hammer was moving up and down steadily, faster than seemed possible. He wore a gray woolen skullcap. Strands of unruly brown and gray hair poked their way out from under the cap in all directions. A leather smith's apron partially covered the sleeveless linen tunic he wore. His arms, massive as small tree trunks, overpowered the edges of the tunic. From the waist down, he wore short leather pants and simple sandals. The back of his right leg was covered with scar tissue.

The forge's fire was being maintained by a fire imp; twin, to Anise's eyes, to Iggy. As they walked into the chamber, the creature was breathing flames onto the coals. Iggy launched himself off Anise's shoulder with another chirp and flew across the room.

5

Iggy chirped several more times as he flew across the broad cavern. The smith didn't notice. He just kept pounding his hammer into the iron on his anvil. The other fire imp did, however. It launched itself into the air also and streaked out to meet Iggy. The bright fire of the forge immediately dimmed.

The two imps met in mid-air. Anise wasn't sure at first what she was seeing as she watched them start to spiral around each other. An intricate aerial dance that could have been fighting, love, or just excitement formed. First, one imp, then the other, flipped, dove, and spun around.

The smith hadn't noticed the chirping or the fire imp leaving the forge. What he did notice, however, was the cooling of the forge fires. He went to reheat his workings, found the fire dimmed, and looked up to see the dance that Anise was watching in fascination.

"Magnus T. Fire Imp," he bellowed.

The dance stopped. One of the fire imps flew, apologetically, over toward the smith. Anise couldn't tell them apart. She felt like her inability to recognize Iggy was some kind of betrayal. Iggy stayed in the middle of the room, flapping his wings.

Anise stepped forward to stand just behind the flapping fire imp. The smith took notice of her for the first time. The other fire imp, Magnus, Anise concluded, landed on the smith's shoulder. "Scorch," said Magnus.

Iggy shook his head. "Burn," he said definitively.

The smith frowned. He looked Anise up and down. "And, who," he said, "might you be?"

"My name is Anise, sir," said Anise.

"Oh, right," said the smith. His annoyance faded. He smiled at Anise. "You're here to pick up your order."

"My order, Sir?" said Anise. "I'm pretty sure I didn't place an order with you."

The smith frowned. "I remember the name," he said. "That's not the sort of thing I forget." He turned and started toward the workbench against one wall. He walked with a pronounced limp. "Let's check the paperwork."

Anise followed.

Magnus, from the smith's shoulder, gave Iggy a once-over. "Burn," said Iggy.

"Scorch?" said Magnus.

The smith started moving iron tools and other things around on the top of the workbench. "Where is it?" he muttered. Some of the things he picked up and tossed casually aside looked intriguing to Anise. There was a glowing two-handed sword, a shield with the face of a bull that winced as it fell to the tabletop, and various things that looked golden or jeweled.

"Aha," said the smith as he pulled a brown leather-bound book from the jumble, "here we are." He opened the book and ran his finger down the open page. "Right," he said. "Your order is not to be picked up; it's for a later delivery." He read a little further. "And I guess you're right. You didn't order the armor; it was ordered for you."

The smith put down the book. He questioned Anise with his eyes. "So why are you here?" he asked.

"I'm afraid I have no idea," said Anise sadly. "Armor, Sir?"

The smith put a kindly, brawny hand on Anise's shoulder. "Well," he said, "I guess you'd best be on your way, then." He snapped his fingers, the cave walls started dissolving, and Anise felt the stone floor begin to fragment beneath her feet.

"Scorch," said Magnus in farewell.

6

Anise wasn't able to get her feet beneath her smoothly. She slipped and fell backward. A surge of anger went through her. *I'm getting tired of all this falling*, she thought. She was sprawled on a perfectly flat green grassy lawn. Beside her was a row of purple flowers, almost identical. The green grass stretched off to the horizon. The horizon was a green wooded hillside. It looked like a painting. Anise rose to her feet.

She strode forward and knocked on the wooden door of the little stone-walled cottage that was the only thing there except for the flowers. She caught a glimpse of Cole's head peeking out of the window. After a moment, the door opened, and he stood there smiling at her.

"Anise," he said cheerily. "I'm so happy to see you. I'm so glad you could drop by. Would you like some tea?"

Anise frowned. "I'd like some answers," she said.

Cole didn't seem to notice her frown or her tone. He dropped his head and whispered quietly, "What did you think of the grass and the hills?" He lifted his head again and continued in a louder voice, "and, do you know how to make tea?"

Anise pushed past Cole into the cabin. It looked the same as it had, except there was a kettle of boiling water and a tea service on the table between the two chairs in the center of the room. She stepped over to the table and poured the hot water from the kettle into the teapot.

"Can you tell me why I keep falling and can't remember anything from before I land?"

"Well," said Cole, "The distances between the way-stops in the dream realm are sleep. You're falling asleep, and when you're sleeping, you don't remember anything except your dreams, isn't that right?"

The hot water started seeping into the herbs in the teapot. The smell of warm chamomile filled the room. Anise felt it relaxing her. Chamomile was her favorite.

"Who's deciding where I go?" she asked. "Can I do anything about it?"

Cole looked thoughtful. He reached up and started playing with his short curly brown hair. "Well," he said, "I think you were ready to drop before you fell asleep." He started winding the hair above his forehead around his index finger. "Also, I don't think you can swim against the dream." He shook his head. "No, that one's not right. What I meant to say was, you're getting a lot of beauty sleep, so you're going to be even prettier when you wake up."

Anise poured the tea into cups, settled back in the rocking chair, and took a slow sip. "You're not being very helpful," she said.

"No?" said Cole. "I'm not?"

The tea was very soothing. Anise struggled to keep her eyes open. "I can't be falling asleep in a dream," she muttered.

Cole winked at her. "You've been doing nothing else," he said.

The rocking chair, the room, and Cole broke into a myriad of shattered dreams, and Anise felt herself falling once more.

HADES

1

Anise landed with a thunk on an inlaid marble floor. She was in an ornate throne room. Rows of people lined both sides of the vast chamber, each of their heads turned toward her. There were entrances on all four walls, including an immense closed double door behind her. There were no windows in the walls, though they were covered with detailed engravings of fields, mountains, and hills.

A raised dais was at the far end of the room with a large ebony throne. In front of the throne stood a man. He had his hand on the collar of a dog. After the crowds turned their heads toward Anise, they turned toward the man. He met Anise's eyes and made a beckoning gesture with his free hand.

Anise walked cautiously down the center of the hall toward the dais. She didn't see that she had any other choice. She looked from side to side as she made her way. Many of the people in the room had an unusual blue pallor on their faces. They were watching her walk with varying degrees of interest.

Anise gasped when she recognized several faces among the crowd. Lyssa and her herders were there. The herders stared at Anise. The anger on their faces felt almost like hunger. Lyssa grinned widely enough that it seemed her face might snap in two. Anise wondered again how she had ever mistaken that look for friendliness.

Anise reached the base of the dais. The man standing there was, of course, Lord Hades. Cerberus was the dog holding under his hand. Each of her three heads was gazing at Anise. One was panting a little, one was tilted a bit to one side, and the third was staring at her intently.

Anise bowed deeply. She knew that you weren't supposed to say Hades' name so as not to draw his attention, though, considering the situation, she thought that maybe that ship had sailed. "My Lord, keeper of the underworld, I crave your indulgence," she said.

Hades towered over her. In addition to being on the dais, he was larger than he had any right to be. Though, as a god, perhaps he had some rights that others didn't have. He was dressed in a gray mantle. His head was covered in thick curly black hair streaked with silver. Leaning against the dark wooden throne behind him was a bident scepter.

Anise glanced past the tall god and spotted a hand waving among the crowd below the dais. It was Cole. He waved a friendly greeting with a smile on his face.

"Anise," said Lord Hades conversationally. "Is it that time already?"

2

L ord Hades and Anise walked side by side through an orchard. He had motioned the throne room crowds to silence and had taken her through a small door behind the throne with hardly a word. After walking down a few marble-floored hallways, they had emerged into a vast open space lined with seemingly endless rows of fruit trees.

Cerberus padded silently beside them. One of her heads sniffed at Anise for a pocket with a treat. Another looked watchfully down the long rows of trees, and the third gazed faithfully at her master.

The sky overhead was a uniform gray, without a cloud or a sun. Anise saw a flock of some distant flying creatures winging by far overhead. They didn't look like birds; they looked more angular and less feathered.

When they first stepped out into the orchard, she had looked carefully at the trees. Though she couldn't imagine the amount of labor it would take to maintain an orchard of this size, they were well looked after. Ripe pomegranates hung low from the branches.

Finally, Hades spoke. Anise gazed up at him, hopeful that he would tell her something to help her understand what was happening to her.

"Anise," said Poseidon's brother, the lord of the underworld, the eldest son of Cronus and Rhea. "I've been expecting you." He held his bident scepter in his right hand. He leaned on it as he walked. He frowned a little, "Though I have to say, I don't enjoy seeing the living down here. There's been a little too much of that going on lately."

"My lord," said Anise, "am I in Hades, or am I in the realm of dream, dreaming I'm in Hades?"

"Yes," said Hades, "you are." The keeper of souls

wrinkled his nose. "There's something about the smell you people have while you're still alive." He sneezed.

Anise sniffed. She could smell nothing but the fruit on the pomegranate trees.

"Anyway, Anise," said the brother of Zeus, "We'll talk more later." They approached a small ramshackle wooden hut under one of the trees. "There's someone here who's desperate to meet you." The grim lord of the dead frowned. "I could almost say she's been dying to meet you if I wanted to be funny, which of course, I don't."

Lord Hades opened the door of the small hut.

Anise hesitated before stepping through the door. She firmed up her resolve. "My lord," she said almost angrily. "How could you take Twilight? He was so young."

"Twilight has not been here yet," said the unseen god. "Though some around him have. Now, go on in. She's been waiting. She refuses to visit the judges until she gets something off her chest."

Anise stepped through the door. One of Cerberus's heads gave her pocket one last disappointed sniff as she walked inside.

3

The interior of the hut was dark and dingy. The rickety wooden door thudded against the frame as Lord Hades closed it from the outside. Anise jumped. The darkness felt complete until her eyes adjusted to it a little bit, then she saw slivers of light filtering in through cracks in the walls. They cast lines of vision across the contents of the room. A slight creaking sound eased into Anise's attention.

She looked around the small space. A bed was against one wall, and a table was against another. An old woman in a rocking chair sat in front of her. The creaking sound was the woman rocking gently back and forth.

"Hello?" said Anise. She didn't dare speak loudly, so she said the word in a whisper. The old woman was looking down at the floor. She wore a shawl around her shoulders and didn't turn to look at Anise. As far as Anise could tell in the dim light, her face was the same bluish color as some of the people's faces in the throne room had been. It was both blue and blotchy. The pallor wasn't uniform.

"Anise?" the woman asked. Anise revised her opinion of her age. Her voice had an air of distraction, but it didn't sound like an old woman's voice.

"Do I know you?" asked Anise.

"No," said the old woman, "though I know you." She shook her head, still gazing fixedly at a spot on the floor. "I see you clearly. Even more clearly now that I am here in the netherworld." She turned her face toward Anise. Her gaze was focused somewhere outside the hut. Milky white clouds of cataracts marred her eyes.

Anise got a little irritated. "Look," she said. "if you have something to tell me, just tell me. I'm getting tired of all this mystery. So, who are you?"

"My name doesn't matter," said the woman. "I was a student at the Academy, like you. Some number of years ago."

Anise revised her estimate of the woman's age down again. The rocking chair and the woman's manner had fooled her. Without the blue pallor and the dark room, she might have looked not much older than Anise herself.

"I was a student at the Academy," continued the woman. "I was trying to learn to walk the paths. The Path of Life, the Path of Death, the Path of the Truth."

Anise scrutinized the woman. She suddenly was full of sympathy for her. Her voice sounded strained. It was like she felt all the world's pain and was trying to bear it for everyone.

The woman continued. "No one knew how to do it. I could find the paths, but no one knew how to help me walk them. But, there was one man who tried to help. One master who thought what I was doing was important."

It suddenly dawned on Anise, who she was talking to.

"Master Lorenzo tried to help me, but he didn't understand. Anise, he got them all wrong. He got my visions, my truths, all wrong."

4

The dead woman gazed through Anise with her sightless eyes. "Master Lorenzo tried to help me while I was alive. But then, after I was gone, he became obsessed with what I had seen, with what I had prophesied." She turned her blind gaze away from Anise and back toward the floor. "I didn't see how he was reading my words until after I had left the world above."

Anise thought for a second about Master Lorenzo. He was the one who had pushed her. The headmaster of the channeling department at the academy, he was supposed to help the students. A wave of bitter anger flooded her. Her Uncle Sebastian had given him a piece of his heart back when he was the Knight of Moon & Shadow. He should have been reformed, but he was the one who had trapped her in this nightmare of dream. "What did your prophecies say?" she asked. "And, what does it have to do with me?"

"I foretold the coming of a powerful channeler. I foretold the existence of a dark channeler, a channeler of death and doom." Her voice grew louder as she spoke. It developed a pitch and timber that made it feel like it was cutting through the gloom in the hut and shaking the walls. "I foretold that the dark channeler would bring doom upon the world. A doom that threatens to shatter and crack existence itself into fragments." She rose to her feet and turned her blind gaze upward as if she could see through the hut's roof. "I foretold that our world would end in a cataclysm of dragon fire, wizard battles, and splintered reality if something wasn't done."

Anise gazed at her. "What does that mean? And, again, what does that have to do with me?"

The woman turned at the sound of Anise's voice. She moved hesitantly toward where Anise was standing. "I tried to get him to listen. I tried from here. I tried to get him to channel me into his dreams, so I could tell him he was wrong. To tell him how he was wrong. But he wouldn't listen. He wouldn't talk to me."

The blind woman was moving too close to Anise. Anise put out her hand toward the woman to hold her at a distance.

"You," she said. "You are the powerful channeler from my prophecy." She reached out her bony finger toward Anise. Her hand was blue and blotchy, like her face. The finger touched Anise on the forehead. Her touch felt cold, clammy, and forceful. "You are the one marked by the silver of the moon and the gold of the sun." Anise felt a force fly from the bony finger on her forehead, into her scalp, and across to the back of her head. She fell back and scrambled toward the door.

The woman stopped, stepped backward, and reached out for her rocking chair. Her voice returned to something approaching normal. "Master Lorenzo read it wrong; he heard it wrong. There were two channelers in my prophecy. The dark channeler and the powerful channeler. He thought there was only one who was both dark and powerful. He's been looking for the powerful channeler, you, because he thinks he will save the world by stopping you."

Anise stood and shook herself. Her scalp tingled. "So, if he's wrong and I'm not the dark channeler who's endangering the world," she said. "Who is?"

The woman looked sad. "I am afraid that master Lorenzo has taken on that role," she said. "Anise, you have to stop him."

5

The woman, subdued now, started rocking again in her chair. "Anise," she said. "I'm tired. I wonder if you could help me." Once again, she turned her sightless eyes in Anise's direction. "I've been waiting for you. I put off going to the underworld judges because I needed to talk to you first. Now I'm done." She held out her arm.

Hesitantly, Anise reached out to help her stand. She waited to feel the same force when she touched the woman's arm, but it didn't come. "How am I supposed to stop Lorenzo?" she asked. "And, what is he doing that could destroy the world?" The woman rose, with Anise's help, to her feet.

"I don't know," she said. "He's doing something or going to do something that is cracking reality. He's fracturing creation." She frowned. "The only other thing I can tell you is that it has something to do with the dragons."

They shuffled together to the door of the little hut. The woman breathed a sigh. "It's been hard," she said, "waiting. But, now, at last, I'm free to go."

Anise opened the door. Hades and Cerberus were still standing outside. Or, perhaps they were standing there again. Anise didn't know. She and the woman, arm in arm, moved across the threshold.

Cerberus bounded forward. She seemed conflicted. Her central head started barking fiercely at Anise. The one on the left dropped toward the ground and whined apologetically. The head on the right tried to lick her.

"Cerberus," called out Hades. All three heads turned, and the dog started walking back toward her master. Hades stepped forward. He held out an arm toward the woman. "Thank you, Anise," he said. "I'll take it from here." The woman took his arm and released Anise's.

Hades turned his eyes to the dog, then back to Anise. "Her job is keeping the dead in and the living out, except those with a reason to be here." He nodded apologetically. "I think she likes you, but she knows you shouldn't be here anymore.

"We'll talk again, Anise," he said, "though, not here." He made a small gesture with his bident scepter. The unwelcome sensation of dream fracturing surrounded Anise, and she was falling again.

6

Anise landed off-balance. She almost fell backward before righting herself. She was standing in the line of red-clad women that she immediately recognized as her Academy physical arts class. She hadn't wanted to take the course at first, but it had evolved into one of her favorites. Her Sifu, their teacher, was standing in front of the line of women. Anise was disoriented.

She shook her head. The rest of the red-clad women disappeared. It wasn't her Sifu; it was a woman Anise had never seen before.

Anise looked around. She was wearing the red linen tunic and leggings that had been the required training gear for her physical arts class. However, the rest of what she had thought she had seen was gone. There was no one there except her and the woman, and her Sifu was nowhere in sight. The only other thing that matched Anise's initial impression was that they were in a training hall.

"We'll have to do something about that," said the woman, referring to Anise's lack of balance. "When you fall, no matter how much time you have or don't have, you need to tuck and roll with the fall to keep your equilibrium."

She was tall, helmed, clad in armor, and held a spear and shield. The armor was a combination of metal, leather, and thick cloth. It seemed like it was designed to balance movement and protection. The spear was short, made of some black material, and looked lethal. The shield was golden in color and bore the image of a woman's head with snakes instead of hair on it. Anise tried not to look directly at the shield, as the snakes gave the impression they were writhing and alive.

The armored woman walked over and tapped the side

of her spear against Anise's back leg. "Straighten that one up," she said. "Otherwise, the stance isn't too bad. You've had some training?" She turned her gaze to Anise's face for the first time. Her stormy gray eyes made Anise look away.

"A little," Anise mumbled to the floor.

"Well," said the woman, "You'll have had more than just a little when I'm done with you."

"My lady," said Anise, still looking at the floor, "Are you the goddess Athena?"

"My name doesn't matter," said the woman. "Who I am to you is the person who will get your flabby spirit into shape."

Anise glanced up at the woman's helmeted face. She thought she caught a hint of a smile on the lips just visible under the helmet's edge.

7

Anise didn't quite manage to stick the landing. Athena had emphasized dropping and rolling to recover quickly after a fall in their training sessions. It allowed you to keep your momentum and maintain your defense if an opponent was present. *I'll get it next time*, she thought.

She was on a trail between dry hills in the Dry Lands again. *I've been here before.* Anise was confused. *I've been here before*, she remembered, *But how many times and for how long?* The times all blurred together. Anise started off down the trail.

A mountain ahead was taller than the hills on the sides of the trail. Anise felt like she recognized it. *I've been trying to get to that mountain*, she recalled. She felt like she saw a spot of green on the distant slopes.

"Burn," said Iggy wearily. He started flapping off along the trail toward the mountain.

"Wait for me, Iggy," said Anise. She ran after him.

Anise hoped that if she reached the mountain and started to climb it, she might get an overview of the brown hills. She thought she'd be able to see if there were other destinations or places to head towards in this dry landscape.

After walking a while, they came to a junction in the trail. Anise stopped. *I've been that way already;* she thought about the left path. She set off along the right one.

The path wound through the trees. Anise wasn't thirsty, although she thought that she should be.

"Have we been here before, Iggy?" Anise asked.

"Burn," said Iggy in confirmation.

8

Anise dropped and rolled as Pallas Athena had taught her. The gravel of the pathway felt rough on her shoulder as the roll carried her into a fighter's crouch. A fighter's crouch, but with no opponent and no weapons. Anise straightened and looked around her.

Her sleeping fall through the Dream realm had brought her, this time, to a fog-shrouded gravel pathway in a barren landscape. The lighting was a uniform gray. She felt like there would be things to see off the sides of the path if the fog wasn't so dense. The place felt a little familiar, though she couldn't precisely place it.

The pathway went two directions, the way she was facing and behind her. Anise started walking carefully forward.

After a few minutes of walking, she spotted two shapes coming toward her through the fog. One was the shape of a tall man, the other a smaller creature walking beside him. She stopped and waited a moment, unsure what to expect.

The man stepped out of the fog, the murky shape resolving into the gray mantle, silver-streaked black hair, and bident scepter of Hades, the lord of the underworld. He wore a golden belt, with a massive key ring covered with keys hung on it. Cerberus bounded into sight beside him. She charged over to Anise, and one of her heads started licking Anise's face. Another kept a watchful eye on Hades to see if he would call her back. The third sniffed Anise for a treat.

"Anise," said Lord Hades, "I said we would talk again. So, here we are."

Anise patted Cerberus on a head. "Where is here?" she said with a glance into the fog.

Lord Hades frowned. "I selected this as a place to meet

because I thought it might be more comfortable for you. This is the Isle of the Wise." He gestured to one side as if there was something to see.

Anise looked around again. "The Isle of the Wise." *No wonder it had looked a little familiar to her.* The little island in the lake off the shores of the Academy had always been a place of mystery. Still, she had visited it a few times with Master Callum during her channeling classes. "I can't say that I've been here that often," she said.

One of Cerberus's heads found a stick on the side of the path. The other two immediately grabbed at it with their mouths, and a three-way wrestling match started.

"Maybe you know," Anise continued. "We never got a straight answer out of master Callum. What is this place? And, how does it connect with the realm of Dream?"

Lord Hades looked thoughtful. "The Isle of the Wise is a thin spot, a fragile patch, in the fabric that separates dream from waking." He nodded sagely. "The isle itself is actually in the realm of Dreaming."

Cerberus fell to the ground, her three necks writhing as her heads battled over possession of the stick.

"But, you can see it from the shores of the lake," said Anise.

"As I said, it's a thin spot. Thin enough that you can see through it. It's old. Older than the Academy." Hades continued, "In fact, the Academy's founders recognized its power. That's why they built the Academy here."

9

Lord Hades gazed at Anise thoughtfully. "But," he said, "that's not what I'm here to talk to you about." He hesitated a moment. The look of hesitation didn't seem to fit on his forceful face. "I need your help, Anise."

Cerberus was still rolling on the ground beside the gravel path. One of her heads yipped, another growled.

"My help?" said Anise. "How could I possibly help the lord of the underworld?"

"Well," said the ruler of the dead, "There are rules. I am limited in some ways as to what I can do directly in the waking world. An agent, or intermediary, can sometimes be necessary."

Anise looked skeptical. "You want me to kill for you? To bring more souls to the nether world?"

Lord Hades looked hurt. "Why does everyone always assume that. I'm not all about killing." He looked contemplative. "You're all coming down to me sooner or later, anyway."

"Then, what?"

One of Cerberus's heads had won the battle for the stick. She stood, and that head shook it forcefully from side to side. The other two looked jealous.

"The clairvoyant you spoke with," said Lord Hades, "I've confirmed what she predicted with other sources. There is a doom coming to the world above. Cracks are forming. Something needs to be done."

"And if the world shatters, your supply of new souls will be cut off," said Anise quietly.

Lord Hades looked a little taken aback. "Well, yes," he said, "But, there are other reasons."

"Uh-huh," said Anise.

"Anyway," continued Lord Hades, "They will call you the Daughter of Death. They will fear you. I will give you a symbol to bring fear to your enemies." He reached out and touched Anise on the forehead. The graveled roadway beneath her feet started to crack.

Cerberus held up her stick for Anise to admire as she began to fall.

10

Anise caught herself, though she didn't do the roll Athena had taught her. She caught herself as she landed astride an animal. She recalled learning to ride with her Uncle Sebastian, then she flailed wildly not to lose her grip. There were no saddle, no reins, and the creature felt wider than a horse. She grabbed the nearest thing she could find to hold onto and breathed a sigh of relief as she got a firm grip with both hands on something rough, scaly, and moving.

She was sitting astride a large reptilian winged creature. She was perched just behind the wings and had a grip on the junction where the wings joined the body. The wings were flapping up and down, and Anise felt a night breeze blowing past her face.

She was riding a dragon. Anise felt a surge of adrenaline. She remembered the chapters in the *Archipelago of Dream*, the book she had read for master Huginn back at the Academy during her clairvoyance classes. The author had described riding on a dragon. Then she realized that this memory was even more appropriate than she had thought. Not only was she riding on a dragon's back, as he had described, but the setting was exactly the same.

The dragon wheeled a bit to the right. Anise clamped down her grip on her hold on the dragon's wings and took in the view.

The sky overhead was similar to the dry gray sky of the Dry Lands but darker. Anise wasn't sure how night could fall in a land without a sun or moon, but it had. The surface far below was a uniform black, marked here and there by white points of light. It was almost like the sky and ground were reversed. Like they were flying over a field of stars. Except for the randomness of the lights, it all looked the same until she looked forward in the direction they were flying. There was something there, on the ground, something more complex and patterned than the simple points of light.

Anise wondered how she could be on the dragon's back without it knowing she was there. She only wondered briefly because as soon as she had the thought, the dragon turned its long serpentine neck, twisted back towards her, and fixed her with its gaze. *It has something in common with Iggy*, Anise thought; *it has cat's eyes*. Then she noticed the expression in those eyes and on that face. It reminded her of Lyssa's herders; it was pure and simple fury.

11

The fury in the creature's eyes stopped Anise's heart. First, she was scared, then she was shamed, then she got angry herself. She met the dragon's gaze head-on. The creature kept flying straight forward with its neck turned towards her. *What have I ever done to you?* she thought.

What haven't you done? The thought entered Anise's head as if she had thought it herself, but she hadn't.

What was that? Anise thought.

You and your kind have broken the pact. You're breaking the world. You've restarted the war. The dragon's eyes burned into Anise's. The intelligence behind those eyes fed the anger.

I haven't done any of those things, thought Anise. *What is this? Who are you?*

You knew me as Flambé, came the voice in Anise's head. *You could not say my real name; you could not understand my real name; I do not want you to know my real name.*

Anise tried to recall where she might know the name Flambé from. At first, nothing came, then she remembered a visit to a carnival when she, Sebastian, and Briac were traveling together years ago.

I haven't done anything to you, she thought.

Look upon the works of your kind and despair. The dragon dove, giving Anise a view of the structure or pattern she had glimpsed in front of them. She held tight to the dragon's wings and looked. It was a vast, roughly round spider web of lines or scratches in the dark surface below. They were all gravitating out from a central point. The lines were colored bright white as the dots or points she had noticed before. There were dots of white scattered between the lines.

At first, it looked like a spider's web to Anise. Some of the lines were brighter, some dimmer, but all glowed white. Then her perception of the pattern changed. Not a spider's web, but instead the pattern of cracks that would show on a frozen lake in winter when someone stepped in the wrong place, and the ice started to fracture. She saw the pattern as the cracks in the clear surface just before the ice expanse shattered, and the walker fell into the frigid water.

It's always been a weak spot, came the voice in her head again. *The holes don't cause too much damage, but the lines, the paths, they score, they splinter.*

The dragon started bucking like a horse trying to throw its rider.

Anise held on for a moment, but the force was too great, and she was thrown. As she plummeted toward the spider web of cracks far below, she felt one more thought intrude into her mind.

If I meet you again in the waking world, came the thought, *I will kill you.*

12

Anise was falling again, but it was different this time. She remembered why she was falling. She remembered what had happened right before her fall. She remembered everything: Master Lorenzo had pushed her. *No, that wasn't right.* She had been riding a dragon, and it had bucked her off.

The dry air rushed up past her. She looked down at the spider's web of cracks and dots looming quickly closer. There wasn't much time before she hit something. She wasn't sure what she was going to hit, but she didn't think it would be pleasant, whatever it was.

Anise focused on one of the bright white dots. She recognized it. It was a circle of light. It was a channeler's circle of light seen from above. They all were. She felt them with her mind. She reached out to them. She knew that she could grab one of them and pull herself through into the waking world.

Anise remembered when master Callum had tried to rescue her by pulling her through his circle of light. She remembered how it had hurt and how she knew it would kill her. She wasn't sure she had much choice.

Thinking her goodbyes to her Aunt Rose, Aunt Isabel, and Uncle Sebastian, Anise prepared to try to pull herself through the nearest circle of light. She hesitated. There was another one. Not the closest, but it was calling to her.

Anise reached out to this new circle of light. It felt welcoming; it felt like home. She caught a whiff of the scent of herbs. The glow of light was coming from a group of clay lamps. Anise grasped this new circle of light like a drowning man clutching for a floating branch. She pulled herself through.

The sight of a room in an infirmary greeted her as she fell asleep and finally woke up.

THE ACADEMY

1

Anise thought about opening her eyes. Then she thought about thinking about opening her eyes. She shifted her body. Was that the feeling of lying between clean sheets in a bed? She felt like she'd forgotten that feeling. She heard a gasp. Then she did open her eyes. A young blond woman was leaning over her. Maybe in her early twenties. Not much older than Anise herself.

"Anise?" said the woman cautiously.

Anise opened her mouth. She licked her lips; her mouth felt dry as dust. *Of course,* she thought, *I've been in the Dry Lands.*

The blonde woman hurriedly grabbed a clay cup of water and held it toward Anise.

Anise attempted to sit up. She felt weak and struggled a bit. Holding the cup awkwardly in one hand, the woman tried to help her with the other.

"Are you Aphrodite?" said Anise.

The woman laughed. She arranged a pillow behind Anise so she could sit up more comfortably. "I wish," she said. "Thank you, Anise." She shook her head. "My name is Aela."

The process of sitting up and leaning against the pillow took all of Anise's concentration. Her body didn't seem to be responding to her thoughts the way it should. She felt heavier and weaker than she remembered. She looked around the room when she was situated relatively comfortably.

There was sunlight streaming into the room from a row of high open windows on the far wall. The sunlight stretched into the room across the tiled floor but didn't quite reach the bed where Anise was lying. Her bed was one of six beds with clean linen sheets and covers in the room. The other beds were empty.

There were lit clay lamps arranged on side tables around her bed. The room smelt like herbs. It smelled a little bit like Lilith's house back in Hero had always smelled to Anise. She took a deep sniff of the fragrant scents. It felt like she hadn't smelled anything in years.

"Where am I?" said Anise. She lifted the clay cup to her lips. The cup felt heavier than it looked. Her arm and hand as she lifted the cup looked different. The cool water felt like heaven as it moistened her mouth and flowed down her throat.

"We're in the infirmary at the Academy," said Aela. "They've been taking care of you here."

"Am I sick?" said Anise. She looked down at her body under the linen bed covers. She didn't feel sick, though something felt wrong or different.

"You're not sick," said Aela. She frowned, "I'm not sure I should be telling you this so soon, but you've been asleep for fifteen years."

I've been falling asleep for fifteen years? Thought Anise.

2

Aela leaned back in her chair and allowed herself a little bit of a self-satisfied smile. "We did it," she said. She smiled at Anise. Anise looked over the circle of little clay lamps, then looked again at Aela.

"What did you do?" she asked. "And who are we?"

"We woke you, of course," said Aela. "Vix and I, we …" She stopped speaking and blushed. Her flushed cheek showed through the wave of blonde hair hiding the side of her face. "I mean the queen. The queen and I came up with a plan to wake you. We heard about The Girl Who Dreamed, and we came up with a treatment plan." She smiled a sort of secret smile. "We will be arguing forever about whether her magic lamps or my herbs did it, but it doesn't matter; it worked."

"The queen?" said Anise. "There isn't a queen. The prince regent isn't married, and if he got married, wouldn't she be a princess regent or something?"

"I'm sorry, Anise," said Aela. "I'm not doing this very well. You have been asleep for a long time. There have been some changes. The prince regent was deposed several years ago. He's locked up in the White Tower."

"So who's the king? Or is there just a queen?"

Aela smiled proudly. "Our good king Twilight. He's the great-grandson of Liam III. People are already saying that they think he's the best king ever."

"Twilight?" said Anise. "The king is named Twilight?"

Aela stood. "I should let you get some rest. Also, I need to tell everyone that you're awake. I'll make sure they don't come in more than one at a time for a while." She frowned. "We'll have to send a message off to Hero as soon as possible, but in the meantime, there are many people around here who will want to see you."

"Who's been coming to see me?" asked Anise.

"Well," said Aela, "I've only been coming here for the last few months, but I heard that some villagers from Hero have made the long trip pretty often. The head of the healing department has been helping with our treatment ideas. Some of your former classmates have visited, I think. A kitchen boy from town has been here a lot." She smiled. "And, of course, master Lorenzo will be excited to hear that you're awake. He's been very interested in the treatment plan, and he's stopped in to see you every few days while I've been here."

If Aela had been looking more closely at her patient as she said this last name, she might have noticed the blood draining from Anise's face.

3

Anise acted quickly after Aela left the room. She wasn't sure how much time she had, but it wouldn't be much. She started by assessing herself, her clothes, and her belongings. She was wearing a simple nightgown, her amulet, and nothing else. There were no clothes near the bed. Other than the beds and the end tables with the clay lamps, the only other furniture in the room was a closed cabinet.

Anise tried to move to the edge of the bed. Her body felt weak and heavy. When she swung her legs over the side, she felt a rush of blood to her head, and she almost fainted. She sat for a moment, breathing heavily.

She considered trying to stand, then decided against it. A more practical means of motion, if less dignified, would be a crawl.

The cabinet was her first target. Painfully, slowly, Anise crawled over to it. She felt old and heavy. She hadn't been in peak physical condition before, though her Sifu, her physical arts teacher, had tried. Now, though, she felt like she hadn't moved in years. For a moment, Anise considered that if she'd really been asleep for fifteen years, the fact that she was moving as well as she was was a minor miracle. She breathed a silent thank-you to the staff of the infirmary.

The cabinet door swung open. It was stuffed with supplies. Anise didn't recognize everything. During her Academy time, there had been a debate about whether or not they should accept healing as a separate discipline. Looking at the unexpected things in this cabinet, Anise thought the healers might have won. There were potions with labels she didn't recognize and devices that looked unfamiliar to her.

One shelf, however, contained herbs and infusions that looked more recognizable. Anise scrambled out some staunchweed, ginseng, mistletoe, and other things. She took a small bit of each herb in her mouth and chewed them to a paste. As she chewed, she thought of Master Ernst and his instructions to carefully measure how much of each ingredient you added to a potion. If he could see her now.

Anise bit her cheek, hard enough to draw blood. The Key to alchemy was, of course, bodily fluids. She sloshed together the ingredient paste she had made with the blood from her bit cheek in her mouth and swallowed.

Anise felt strength flow into her joints. She might feel the repercussions later, but her makeshift concoction was working for now. She stood and looked out the window. It was late afternoon. The sun was lowering toward the horizon. The window was on the first floor and low enough to the ground that she could climb out. There was even a hedge there for concealment.

Anise scrambled out the window and into the shadows behind the hedge. The cool early evening breeze ruffled the bottom edge of her nightgown around her legs.

4

The gray stone outer wall of the Academy rose in front of Anise. It felt like the wall of a cage or a prison for the first time. She had made her way here, her nightgown flapping around her, skulking through the setting sun's shadows. However, the wall was a more formidable barrier than those shadows had been.

Working with the element earth was different than working with fire, water, or air. With fire, you drew on a heat source from somewhere close. If there wasn't a fire to hand, body heat, or the ambient temperature of the air. Water involved pulling moisture from some nearby source. Air was always moving somewhere, and you stilled it in one place with your mind to cause it to move elsewhere.

Earth was different. With earth, you had to dig deep. You had to feel the forces moving beneath your feet to get them to move the way you wanted. Earth work was usually slow. Fortunately for Anise, she was still on Academy grounds. She could still feel the presence of the volcano: the Key to the Elements, roaring and belching fire and lava. The volcano that lived inside the vast Hall of Elements on the Academy grounds flooded her mind with elemental force.

She moved close to the wall and put her hand on the smooth stone. The wall was a seamless expanse of rock above her, formed by some long-ago mage. She let the power of the streaming molten lava of the Key flow through her hand. The smooth stonework started to move and surge under her touch.

Anise shaped a round rabbit hole of an escape tunnel into the stone. She had to reform it a second time to make it a little bigger, as her hips were just a little wider than she remembered. She scampered through and looked to see where she was when she reached the other side.

Her tunnel had opened up into a place just on the outskirts of Ashton. Just between the edge of the town and the beginnings of the soap workings. The soap-makers kept their fires and ash pyres outside of town to keep the smoke and the smells away from citizens who might complain.

The last rays of the setting sun were leaving. Sunset was transiting to twilight. An almost full moon was rising in the sky. Anise felt the warmth of the sunny side of her amulet start to dim and noticed a cool touch on her skin from the silver side.

With the sun leaving the sky, she felt Helios' attention leaving her. Her amulet connected her to the sun god during the day, and his sister, Luna, at night. She didn't hear them speak, but instead, she felt aware of what they could see from the sky above. It had proved helpful during snowball fights with her fellow students back at the Academy. She had acquired the reputation for having eyes in the back of her head. It might prove even more helpful when things got more serious.

She looked toward Ashton. The town felt like home to her. She had lived in Maeve's way-house in Ashton the whole time she was a student at the Academy. She couldn't see much of the town from here. The hill and watchtower of the Dragon's Eye were silhouetted against the sky. The tower on the top of the rise, a familiar sight to her, was surrounded by scaffolding. The Dragon Watchtower was being rebuilt.

Anise shivered a little and pulled her nightgown more tightly around her. She turned away from the Academy and away from Ashton, into the soap works, and toward whatever lay beyond.

5

The air started to grow cold as twilight faded into the night. The glow of the nearly full moon was enough so that Anise didn't have to summon light. In the last year at the Academy, master Videmon had taught his students how to conjure his shining sphere of white and yellow. Anise still wondered if it was somehow a mixture of fire and other elements. Summoning it felt different than producing fire, and it didn't consume wood or other materials like flame did.

Anise shivered as the breeze pressed her nightgown against her body. Soon she was going to need something to keep her warm, as well as something to see by.

She crept through the fields, sheds, and buildings of the soap works. Several competing families had run the town's soap production. After a while, they had seen the value of working together. They had formed a guild and located their businesses in the same vicinity.

Anise avoided guards and lit areas. The businesses mostly ran during the daytime, but they kept the facilities guarded at night. She saw a massive mound of charcoal and wood ash ahead of her. The piles or hearths were kept smoldering to produce the wood ash needed for soap production. The radiant heat from deep inside the mountain of gray and black material warmed her as she started past it.

It was more than just the heat warming her. Anise felt drawn to the black and gray of the smoldering mound. She stopped, rose to her full height from her crouch, and turned to face the ash and charcoal mountain. Anise lost herself for a moment. Something about the pile was drawing her toward it.

She took a step toward the ash and charcoal. The mound's edge pushed aside and around her foot as it approached. She moved a little further. More of the pile shifted around her other foot as it moved into the sooty charcoal. Another step, and then another, and she was waist-deep in the ash. The ash and coal flowed around her body. She encountered no more resistance than a person wading through water.

Anise walked further into the charcoal hearth. After a moment, her head disappeared into the mound. The surface of the ash stirred for a second, then settled.

An owl flew overhead over the undisturbed mountain of charcoal and hooted as it made its way on its nightly hunt.

6

The nearly full moon shone down on the charcoal pile. A passing hedgehog startled and fled into the underbrush as the ash and charcoal on the edge of the heap started shaking and moving. Anise pulled herself out of the black and gray mound. She was covered from head to toe in the product of the charcoal maker's work.

She stepped away from the pile and coughed. She reached up and wiped her face. A smear of gray ash dropped off. As if waking from sleep, Anise looked around herself. There was no one in sight, but she hurried away from the charcoal pile and into the woods. The mound had been at the edge of the soapmaker's workings, and the woods beyond were blessedly free of any signs of people or town.

More gray ash fell off her body as she fled into the woods through the underbrush. The ash fell off, but the black that she had thought was from the charcoal remained. Anise broke through the low growth into a clearing in the forest. She stopped to examine herself by the light of the gibbous moon.

Her nightgown was gone, lost somewhere in the depths of the charcoal pile. She stamped her foot. The last of the gray ash fell off her body. She was clothed from neck to foot in some black material. It felt light. Light enough that she could move freely but strong enough to have protected her from the brambles and branches of the underbrush she had pushed her way through.

There were separate boots, leggings, tunic, and gloves, but they all fit together like tongue and groove fittings in fine carpentry. Clever little snaps and clasps kept the fit tight but could be unfastened to take the suit off. The clothing wasn't just strong; it was warm as well. Anise no longer felt the bite of the crisp night air.

She unclipped the clasps that held on one glove. She tried to stretch the material. She examined it as well as she could by the moon's light. It wasn't linen, it wasn't leather, it wasn't metal, as best as she could tell. She formed a pretty good idea of what it wasn't, which didn't help her much with what it was. She wondered if this might be the armor delivery from the blacksmith in her dreams.

First things first, thought Anise. She snapped the glove back on and oriented herself by the north star through the clear sky over the clearing. She headed off through the woods to the northeast, away from Ashton and away from the Academy.

7

Anise was growing tired of pushing her way through the underbrush. Her miraculous new armor helped with the cold. Still, her makeshift restoration potion was starting to wear off, and she felt tired and weak. She had been walking as directly northeast as she could, orienting herself by the north star whenever she caught a glimpse of the sky through a break in the trees.

The way had been mostly downhill. Ashton, the Academy, and the lake were higher in altitude than the lowlands to the east. Walking to the northeast, Anise was headed toward the sea and the Dragon River. She would somehow have to cross the river if she kept going east. Or else her path would eventually be blocked by the sea.

She broke through the underbrush into a clearing. A stream cut through the clearing, heading down the slope to the northeast, as she was. Anise stumbled to the bank of the stream, fell to her knees, and lowered her face to the cold mountain water. The water was icy and refreshing and brought her back a whiff of alertness.

The gibbous moon lit the clearing enough that she caught a glimpse of herself reflected in a pool of still water at the side of the stream. She didn't recognize her face at first. *An Old woman* was the first thought that reflection brought to mind. *What by god's bones did they do to my hair* was the second. The people taking care of her body at the Academy infirmary hadn't taken too much care of her hair. It was cropped relatively short and straight across, without attention to style. But that wasn't the main thing she noticed. There was something wrong with the color.

Anise held out her hand, palm upward, and conjured a tiny point of master Videmon's light. She got a better look at herself in the reflection on the water's surface. Her face looked older, but she could still see herself in there. Her hair, though, had changed. The color was mostly the same, but a gray or silver streak ran right through the center, from her forehead through to the back. She reached up to touch it. The silver part didn't feel any different than the rest.

Anise shook her head. She was too tired to worry about this right now. The light flickered out, and she looked around the glade. A spot under a bush would be out of sight if anyone entered the clearing. It would be a good place to hide.

Anise blessed the armor keeping her warm and cushioning her body from the hard ground as she curled up into a ball under the bush and dropped off to sleep.

8

The familiar feeling of waking into a dream overtook Anise as she opened her eyes. At first, it was familiar, but then it wasn't. *Wait*, thought Anise, *I'm not falling.* She looked around her. A moonlit clearing next to a rushing stream met her inspection. She reached out with her mind and felt the reassuring presence of her circle of light. She had almost forgotten what a regular channeling dream felt like.

Anise crawled out from beneath the bush she had been sleeping under. She looked around the clearing. The moonlight and the trees circling her defined the edges of her circle of light. She pushed and pulled at it with her mind, ensuring that she had control and could end this dream when she chose. The relief she felt when she was sure she did was almost palpable.

A flapping noise wafted across the space. Anise turned and saw Iggy winging his way across the clearing toward her. She choked up.

"Ig … Iggy, ….," Anise sputtered.

Iggy flew over to Anise, hovered in front of her, then landed on her shoulder. His tail wrapped lovingly around her neck.

Anise reached up and squeezed Iggy's tail. "Where've you been?" she asked.

"Burn," said Iggy calmly, by way of explanation.

9

Anise awoke. Something was different. She didn't have the sensation of falling. She rested, her eyes comfortably closed, and reveled in the feeling of lying on a flat surface. She was comfortable. Her body felt warm and relaxed, and her head felt warm too. In fact, her head felt a little too warm.

She opened her eyes then and shifted her body. Iggy, who had been settled on the ground pillowing Anise's head, sleepily muttered, "Burn?"

Anise sat up and looked around. She was in the clearing by the rushing stream. The sky overhead started shifting from the starry black of night to early morning gray. Iggy blinked. His eyes had vertical slits for pupils, like a cat.

While sleeping, her armor had cushioned her from the hard ground and kept her body warm. Iggy, who burned a small furnace inside himself, had kept her head warm.

She stood and took in the heavens. Iggy flew up and landed on her shoulder. The moon wasn't up, and though the sun's light was just beginning to creep its way into the sky, she could still make out the north star.

An owl called. Instead of thinking that it was just the owl's last call before he settled in to sleep the day away, Anise had the feeling that he was calling to her.

Anise was overcome with a rush of happiness. She was back; she was back in the real world. She had left the world of dreams behind and could continue her life. There might be trials and challenges ahead, but she would face them awake and on her feet. Now, though, it was time to see what that owl wanted.

Anise picked up a short stick from the ground and started beating her way through the underbrush toward where the owl call had come from. It called out again as she made her way. She corrected her path and continued.

The sky she spotted overhead through the trees started to grow lighter still. Anise broke through the underbrush to a spot under a large oak that was a little clearer. There, hanging from a low branch of the tree, was a round black shield with an owl's face outlined in gold on the surface. Anise looked down at the stick she had been using to beat back the underbrush. It was a short sharp spear made of some dark metal.

"Burn," said Iggy with satisfaction.

10

Still using her new spear to clear the underbrush from her path, Anise made her way through the forest. The sun had risen, and she used the occasional glimpses she got of it through the trees for orientation. She kept to her northeast course directly away from the Academy as best she could.

Iggy was planted on her shoulder. Her relief at having a companion in the waking world and, she hoped, a friend was fading as he grew heavier through the morning. He was snoring. The sound was a little like a cross between a car's purr and the rumble of the water mill back in Hero.

The shield with the golden owl on its face gave her a surprise. She had strapped it onto her arm, and it had flickered a bit and then disappeared. With a bit of practice, she had found that she could make it appear and disappear at will.

Anise spent most of that day trekking cross country, using the sun as her guide. She found some berries at one point and nibbled away a little bit of her hunger. She re-encountered the steam she had seen the day before and slaked her thirst. At one point, she made her way across a road. She wasn't sure why, but she carefully waited until she was sure no one was coming before she crossed.

As the sun got to a place in the sky where Anise thought it might be afternoon, she came to a broad river. Anise wasn't that familiar with the geography of this part of Liamec, but from what she did know, this had to be the Dragon River.

The Dragon river wound its way from the mountains to the south and west, cutting the Serpent's Gorge into the rocks. After coming down from the mountains, it turned to the north and flattened out a bit as it made its way toward the ocean.

Anise was relieved to see that the river was smooth and calm here, though wide. She had heard that it got rough and wild as it got closer to the coast.

She made her way down to a river-pebble-covered bank. The far side of the river was forested, but a grassy slope led down to the water's edge. Her thirst had returned. Anise got down on her knees and leaned over the still water to take a sip. Iggy flapped off her shoulder as she approached the river as if he was reluctant to be so close.

Anise caught a glimpse of her reflection as she hovered over the water. She gasped and pulled back. Her body looked right in the reflected image. She saw the black material of her armor and even glimpsed the spear she still held in her right hand. But, her face had been replaced with a skull.

Anise reached up to her face and felt her cheeks. She felt flesh under her fingertips. She looked again into the reflective water. The empty eye sockets of a skull looked back at her.

Anise reached out and carefully put her fingertips into the water. She felt the edges of something solid. She lifted and pulled a solid head-sized object out of the water with a grinning skull's face on the front. It was a helmet.

DEATH'S DAUGHTER

1

The river stretched in front of Anise, wide and deep. She wondered if her new armor was flexible enough to swim in. Then she thought that it didn't matter. Her idea of swimming had been splashing around in the millpond with her friend Mary back in Hero. She wouldn't have ever tried to swim something this wide, even without the armor.

Anise kicked at the smooth river pebbles that covered the beach. She thought about ways she could get across the river. She needed to cross to get further away from the Academy to make it harder for Lorenzo to find her. Then she thought about where she might be going in the longer term. Anise shook her head. That thought was for another time.

"Burn," said Iggy thoughtfully.

"Well, Iggy," said Anise, "that's a good suggestion." She shook her head again. In fact, Iggy's suggestion had given her an idea.

Anise stepped to the river's edge. She held out her hands, palms downward, and drew on the elements. She pulled heat away from the water's surface.

The water on the surface of the river froze almost immediately. The ripples and tiny waves froze in place. It wasn't totally smooth, but it was smooth enough. Anise expanded the scope of her action and started crafting a path of ice away from the pebble beach.

"Burn," said Iggy resentfully when he felt the cold. He flapped off her shoulder and took off into the air above her.

Anise took her first step onto her ice pathway. The ice shifted a bit under her weight, so she directed a bit more heat away from under the top layer. She kept one hand palm down toward the ice and faced the other upward toward where Iggy was flying. She conducted the heat she was pulling away from the water up in Iggy's direction.

"Burn," said Iggy gratefully. He started doing flips and aerial maneuvers in the warm updraft.

Anise froze the water in front of her for her next step. She felt grateful for the boots in her armor, as they were insulated well enough that her feet didn't feel the cold. She thought about the water flow, the depth of the river, and how much water she would have to freeze.

It didn't matter. Anise let the ice behind her warm and kept the ice under her feet cold enough and frozen enough so that it didn't shift when she stepped on it. When she needed to freeze it more, the additional blast of heat that she released into the air sent Iggy into spasms of joy.

Anise crossed the river. When she reached the other side, she stopped, took a deep breath, and flopped down on the grassy bank for a rest. Iggy flew down and landed on the grass beside her.

The fire imp looked behind them, across the river, over the bits of drifting ice. Iggy launched himself urgently back into the air, his wings flapping hard. He coughed out a quick burst of flame, turned his catlike eyes to Anise, and called down to her in warning, "Burn!"

2

There was something large and dark standing on the other side of the river. Standing on the river pebble beach that Anise and Iggy had come from. The sun was setting behind the shape, and the river was wide, so Anise had difficulty making out exactly what it was. She could tell it was big, however. It was probably about twice the height of a man.

Iggy started hissing and spitting like a kettle that needed to be taken off the stove. Anise watched the shape, unsure what it was or what it was doing there. At first, it just stood there. It was facing toward where Anise and Iggy were. Anise tried to look at the shape carefully through the bright light of the setting sun. There was something familiar about it.

The shape moved. It took a step forward toward Anise's side of the river. It didn't take precautions or make any preparations; it just started walking into the water. Anise started. She had felt relatively safe with the broad expanse of water between her and whatever it was. She wasn't so sure anymore.

The shape waded into the water like a child wading into a puddle. The slow water near the pebble beach didn't slow it down, and the faster water further away from the shore didn't affect it either.

Anise had hopes for the depths near the center of the river, and in fact, as the shape approached that point, the creature slowed a bit. Anise felt relieved when it totally disappeared under the fast-flowing river water.

Her relief faded when the setting sun's light reflected off of an unwavering moving arrow of v-shaped ripples that advanced right toward her.

Iggy hissed the entire time. The sound grew steadily louder. Anise worried that he might hurt himself.

"Enough of this, Iggy," said Anise urgently, "Come on." She stood, turned, and started scrambling up the grassy wooded slope behind her. She thought, *there is no reason to just stand and wait for it, whatever it is.*

3

Anise fought her way up the forested slope. At the top, there was a clear space. She stopped for a second to catch her breath. Iggy flapped off above her and turned to look behind them. The open space was the cleared area at the side of a road. Some major thoroughfares in Liamec were kept clear on both sides to make it harder for bandits to surprise travelers and prevent the routes from being overgrown.

This roadway was such a thoroughfare, though there was no traffic right now. It ran north/south, paralleling the river.

"Burn," said Iggy sadly.

Anise turned to look back in the direction he was looking. She couldn't see anything, not having Iggy's high vantage point, but she heard a loud crashing sound. It sounded like a tree falling. *Is it strong enough to just knock the trees over?* She thought.

If it's already at the bottom of the wooded slope, then it's gaining on us, even with having to ford the river.

She darted across the road, then crossed the cleared area on the other side. She found a spot behind some bushes where she could hide. The thundering sound of trees falling continued from the other side of the roadway. It seemed like it was knocking over everything in its way as it crashed up the wooded slope.

In less time than she would have thought possible, the creature, whatever it was, knocked over another tree and stepped out onto the space beside the road. It was close enough now that she could see it plainly, though, in some ways, its appearance was still confusing.

Anise recognized it. It was her worst fear; it was a

nightmare brought to life. It was death and destruction, walking on two feet. It was at least ten feet tall and an indeterminate gray color.

Anise recognized it and felt a rush of despair. From what felt like an eternity ago, she remembered how her uncle had become the Knight of Moon & Shadow and defeated an identical monster. The creature had been summoned by Lorenzo to attack their village. Her uncle had fought the beast using the magical gifts he had borrowed from his fellow villagers and his father's sword. It was a nightmare, a dream beast, twin to the one that had killed her parents.

4

The beast stepped out onto the roadway and then stopped. It was facing right toward where Anise was behind a bush at the far edge of the cleared ground. It stopped and waited for something. Anise remembered when she saw a creature like this step into the Hero town square and stand precisely this way.

Tears came to her eyes. At that time, she had been sure, confident that her Knight of Moon & Shadow, her Uncle Sebastian, would defeat the beast, as he had. There was no one here but her this time, and she was hiding behind a bush.

The tears weren't just for her, however. She remembered how that creature had left her an orphan. She remembered who had summoned that beast and who had most likely channeled this one as well.

The tears stopped flowing. Anise took a firm grip on her spear. She let her shield flicker in and out of existence to ensure it was still there. She checked the buckles on her boots and gloves. The fading tears turned to anger, then the fading anger turned to rage.

It must have been Lorenzo that had summoned this beast. He had pushed her into the nightmare of fifteen years of Dream. He had bragged about overcoming her uncle's attempt to give him a piece of his heart. And now, he was going back to his old tactics and summoning death dreams to attack her. She had had enough.

Anise conjured a bright ball of master Videmon's light, gripped her spear more tightly, stepped out from behind her bush, and strode toward the creature.

The light drifted up and to one side, illuminating the clearing alongside the roadway and overpowering the last rays of the setting sun.

Anise reached up to her head and pulled the visor of her death's visage helmet down over her face. The ghostly image of a skull on the front of the helmet almost glowed in the white light.

Iggy flew alongside Anise. "Burn," he said eagerly.

5

As Anise stepped into the cleared space, the beast responded. It moved forward, reared back its head, and roared. The sound was loud. The leaves on the trees lining the sides of the roadway trembled as if in a strong wind.

Anise trembled a bit, too, though her armor hid it. The sound was fear. It fed fear through your ears, across your soul, and into your heart. She trembled, but her rage held firm. With a smooth motion, she lifted her spear above her head, cocked her arm back, made a short approach run, and launched the razor-sharp weapon at the beast.

The creature looked startled as if it had expected its challenge roar to have at least delayed its opponent's attack. Still, with a preternaturally quick motion, it knocked the flying spear to one side. Any human-forged weapon would have shattered with the force of that blow, but the spear was a gift from Athena, goddess of wisdom and war, and it would take more than this to break it. However, the weapon's course was changed, and instead of flying back to Anise's hand, it struck the trunk of a tree behind the beast. The tree trunk shattered, and the spear fell to the ground.

Anise stood, momentarily disarmed. She called her shield into appearance with her thoughts and raised it toward the creature.

Iggy flitted over to where the spear had landed and picked it from the ground. He started flapping back toward Anise with the weapon clutched in his talons.

The beast moved forward. For something so huge, it moved surprisingly quickly.

The formerly empty roadway wasn't empty anymore.

Out of the corner of Anise's eye, she noticed that several carts and other travelers had gathered from both directions. They were stopped, watching her face off with the beast. No one dared approach, but they couldn't tear themselves away from the spectacle.

"What is that thing?" Anise heard someone ask in terrified, hushed tones.

"Do you mean the monster or the woman who looks like she's related to Death?" someone else responded.

Slowed by carrying the spear, Iggy got too close to the creature. It lashed out with one of its limbs. Somehow even this close to the beast, it wasn't clear if it had hands, claws, or tentacles. The limb struck the fire imp, and he crashed to the ground. The spear clattered down beside him.

"Iggy!" called out Anise. She raced forward.

6

The creature stepped over Iggy's crumpled form. Anise realized there was nothing she could do for the fire imp until she had done something about the beast. She dove toward the fallen spear, dropping and rolling in a move Athena had taught her, which should leave her armed and ready at the end of it.

Once again, the creature moved preternaturally quickly. It seemed to know where Anise was moving to before she moved there. Anise could see the blow coming but couldn't shift her momentum fast enough.

"Burn," came a weak voice from below the creature. A blast of fire shot upward from the ground, bathing the beast's legs in flames. It wasn't clear if the fire damaged the beast, but it did distract it. The blow it had been aiming for Anise missed. Her roll completed as planned, with her alert, armed with her spear, and facing the creature.

Anise thought about what to do next. She would have to keep the beast's speed in mind. She couldn't afford to underestimate it again.

A particular smell filled the air. It smelled like something burning. Perhaps Iggy's fire had done some damage. Anise remembered one time when Aunt Rose had left her in charge of the bakery ovens while she ran an errand. Anise had gotten distracted by something, and a day's worth of goods had been burnt to a crisp, leaving their little house smelling like burnt bread. This smell didn't remind her exactly of burnt bread. It reminded her more of seared, rotting meat.

The creature hesitated as if waiting to see what Anise would do next. Anise felt slow. She hadn't regained whatever fitness she had had before her sojourn into Dream. Still, she felt like she knew something about fighting this beast from watching her uncle long ago. And she had confidence in her armor, weapons, and abilities. The armor supported her uncertain muscles, and the shield and spear gave her courage.

Anise was now on the other side of the wide road. The moon showed itself over the horizon behind the creature, and the last rays of the setting sun were bathing its gray front in a ruddy glow. *At least it's got the sun in its eyes*, she thought.

The creature grew tired of waiting. It charged at Anise, lifting one of its limbs over its head in preparation for a devastating blow.

7

Both the moon and sun were in the sky. Anise felt a shift in the knowledge coming to her from her amulet. She could feel the direction and location of the blows the beast was delivering. The source of the awareness was drifting from Helios and the sun to Luna and the moon.

Of course, in this case, she could see the blow, as well as sense it with her amulet. She brought up her buckler and moved to the side as quickly as she could. The beast drove its limb down toward her. The tentacle struck her shield with a glancing blow. Even through the magical protection of the owl's head buckler, Anise could feel the force of the impact. The limb continued downward, smashing into the rocks and gravel of the roadway with a thunderous crash.

Anise heard the people watching gasp. They moved backward to give the combatants more space as the gravel shot out from the impact.

Anise thrust with her spear, holding it near the end to give herself as much length as possible. The creature had a greater reach than her, though, for that purpose, a spear was a better weapon than a sword might have been. She thrust at the nearer of the creature's legs while it was still recovering from its blow. The tip of the spear connected, and a drop of blue blood oozed from the gray skin.

The beast roared again and delivered a furious backhanded swing toward Anise.

Anise thanked her amulet and Helios and Luna for the little bit of foreknowledge the medallion gave her. It gave her a reaction edge that let her compensate for the creature's speed. She ducked just under the swing. She felt the creature's tentacle whistle through the air just above her head.

Reaching her arms outward, Anise conjured flame darts

from the air alongside the beast. As the darting fingers of fire smashed into the creature from both sides, she heard the growing crowd reacting to the cold that surged outward in every direction. Anise had to concentrate on drawing the heat for the flame from the air and not from the crowd's bodies.

The smell of burning rotting flesh grew slightly, and the creature slowed a bit. It took another swing. Anise stepped back and jabbed her spear at the creature's limb as it whistled past. She was rewarded with another drop of blue ichor.

As the creature swung its tentacle backward to prepare another mighty blow, Anise launched her spear at it again. This time the beast was slowed enough that it didn't have time to knock the spear to one side.

In a spurt of blue fluid, the spear struck the center of the creature's chest, buried half its length into its body, and stuck there. The beast stopped and showed an expression that might have passed for surprise on a more expressive face. It started to topple over in Anise's direction, making her worry about whether or not it would hit her. Then, it faded into nothingness, leaving Anise's spear clattering to the roadway in a puddle of the creature's blue blood.

8

The crowd didn't quite know how to react to the beast's defeat. There was a smattering of applause like they had just seen the end of a show, but it was clear that some weren't sure if they had seen a monster defeated or a monster victorious. They didn't know if they should be relieved or scared.

Anise picked up her spear and wiped the blue ichor off it on the grass on the side of the roadway. Some of the crowd, the ones who clapped, started shuffling forward. She turned to face them, stood straight, and spoke. She hadn't spoken with her helmet on before. The mask amplified and changed her voice so much that she almost didn't recognize the loud and powerful sound. She heard gasps from the crowd as they saw the skull on her face, and they heard her augmented voice.

"I am the Daughter of Death," Anise thundered out. "Stay back if you value your lives."

Having hopefully bought a little time before she was interrupted, Anise turned to Iggy.

It almost made her cry to see him. Iggy was lying in a crumpled heap on the gravel of the roadway, his wings twisted beneath him. Like where the beast had fallen, there was a thin puddle of blood beneath him, though the fluid that flowed in his veins was a bright orange color.

Anise leaned over the fire imp. She felt a rush of heat coming from the puddle and the fire imp's body. At first, she thought his spirit was gone, perhaps departed back to wherever he had been channeled from. Then, Iggy opened his eyes and looked up at her. His cat-eye pupils were dilated to almost fully open, perhaps from shock.

Iggy moaned when Anise tried to straighten out his twisted wings. She mumbled, "What am I going to do with you." She shook her head. "What am I going to do for you?"

Iggy opened his mouth. A trickle of the orange ichor ran from a cut on his lip down his chin.

"Burn," he said weakly.

Anise's eye's widened. "Of course," she said. She held her hands over the fire imp's prone body and conjured a searing surge of fire downward. The flames crackled over Iggy's gray leathery skin.

As Anise watched, the wounds and cuts on the creature's body healed. His eyes closed, and he began making a soft sound. Anise didn't recognize the sound until she stopped the crackling flames. It was somewhere between a purr and a snuffle. Iggy had fallen asleep and was snoring.

Marveling at the healing that the flames had done, Anise picked up the slumbering fire imp and slung him over her shoulder. She tried to ignore the crowd of people, still watching her fearfully.

Anise crossed the roadway and disappeared into the trees on the far side without another word.

9

The young king woke from a restless night. He reached out his hand for his queen, his Vix, lying next to him in bed. She wasn't there. He sat up and looked around the room, confused. *Had she gone off on an expedition herb hunting with Aela?*

At first, their bedchamber looked normal, but then he realized that the furniture in the room was missing except for the bed and the night table. There was something wrong with the lighting as well. He couldn't tell if it was night or day.

Twilight rose from his bed in his nightshirt and picked up his dagger from the nightstand. He kept it there mainly for sentimental reasons. He didn't feel the need to keep a weapon around while he slept. Capitol, the capital city of Liamec, had been peaceful and calm since the end of Taedum's Revolt. The smooth wooden handle of the knife felt comfortable in his hand.

The door opened, and a woman stepped through. She was a bit older than the king, perhaps a dozen years. She was dressed in ordinary clothes. He might not have noticed her on the street, except for one thing. Her hair, mainly brown, had a streak of silver that ran down the middle. It drew the eye.

"Excuse me?" said Twilight.

"Twilight," said the woman. "Is it really you?"

"Of course I'm me," said the young king. "More importantly, who are you, and what are you doing in my bedchamber?" Twilight was a bit surprised to see tears in the corners of the woman's eyes. He wouldn't have expected to see such sentiment from an assassin, even a non-threatening one such as this.

"Twilight," said the woman, the tears flowing more freely, "I'm so happy to see you." She stopped, peering at him through the tears in her eyes, and continued, "You've grown into such a fine, strong-looking young man."

"Do I know you?" asked the king. He lowered the dagger he was holding a little.

The woman shook her head. "There's a lot to tell." She looked thoughtful. "First off, this is a dream."

Twilight shook his head in denial. Then he paused, looked around the room, and said, "Strange kind of dream."

She frowned. "I trained at the Academy as a channeler. I guess I can dream-walk as well. Dream-walking is something that some channelers can do. You channel yourself into another channeler's dream." She smiled. The expression lit up her face and made her look very friendly. Twilight found himself liking her, even under the strange circumstances. "Master Callum never said anything about walking into the dreams of non-channelers, but I seem to have done it."

10

The woman continued, speaking eagerly to show him how much she wanted him to believe her. "I'm your sister," she hesitated, "Or maybe your aunt or something. I used to watch you when you were a baby."

"You're not helping your cause much," said the young king. He lifted his dagger again a little. "No one watched me as a baby. I grew up in the woods." He glanced at the carved wolf's head on the hilt of his dagger. "Tell me your name and why you are here. I've never heard of dream-walking. I know a little bit about channeling."

"You must have survived in the woods when they lost you!" she exclaimed. "Did you do that by yourself? You were only two!"

Twilight looked a little unsure. Regardless he repeated, "Your name."

The woman took a breath. "My name is Anise. As I said, I trained at the Academy. ..."

The king interrupted. "Anise. I know that name. Aren't you the one Vix was talking about? The sleeper, the patient at the Academy, The Girl Who Dreamed?"

"I guess so," said Anise. "I guess I must be." She reached out her hand as if to touch Twilight's arm. "But, listen, I may not have much more time. I'm not sure how long I can keep this going. I haven't tried it before."

The young king took a step backward to avoid Anise's touch. "All right," he said. "Let's get back to my question. Why are you here?"

Anise looked sad at his withdrawal. "I wanted to see you. I wanted to see if you were still alive. I thought for so long that you were dead."

"Lots of people have thought that I was dead at various

times. But, so far ... Not so far," said the young king.

"One thing puzzles me, though," said Anise. "How are you, the king?"

"That puzzles me too," said Twilight wistfully.

Anise perked up. "I can take you to meet your parents, Twi," she said.

The young king darted a suspicious glance at Anise. "No one calls me that, except for Vix and a couple of old friends." He changed his tone and said, "I haven't got any parents, except maybe for ..." he looked again at the carved wolf's head on the hilt of his dagger.

"Of course, you have parents," said Anise. The tears that had dried on her cheeks started flowing again. "They'll be so happy to see you."

11

Anise woke up. The birds were just starting their morning chorus. Iggy made a fine pillow in some ways; the warmth of his body kept her head warm, but the rumbling snore was sometimes a distraction, and he wasn't as soft as he could be. She moved her head, and he grumbled in his sleep.

She had made a campfire last night. The remnants still smoldered in her improvised fire pit. After waking from his recuperative rest, Iggy had proven very good at gathering firewood. Her elemental skills had taken care of the fire-starting.

Food had been a little more challenging, but she had remembered some of Lilith's teachings. The cunning woman who helped the mayor run her home village of Hero had taught her before she came to the Academy. The herbal skills Lilith had passed on had been helpful. Anise had found some berries and mushrooms and stumbled across a modest growth of wild parsnip in a stroke of luck. She carefully avoided touching the leaves or stems of the parsnips, remembering Lilith's warnings. Her boots helped knock the plants to the ground, and after hesitation, she used her spear to dig the roots up. She checked the edge afterward and was relieved to see not a scratch on it.

Master Ernst at the Academy had been knowledgeable about the benefit of herbs for brewing potions. Still, Anise went back to Lilith's teachings for foraging. Master Ernst had expected the plants to already be packaged, bottled, or dried.

Anise knew that if she stayed in the wild for long, she would have to do some hunting. For some reason, she felt reluctant to use her Academy skills to trap animals for the hunt. It felt like cheating. Of course, when she got a little more hungry, her reservations would almost certainly fade.

Iggy woke and launched himself into the air. For some reason, the bird song seemed to annoy him. He blew a thin stream of fire in the direction the sound was coming from. The blast of flame made a crackling noise in the air. Even though the fire didn't reach them, the noise and heat made the closer birds stop singing.

"Iggy," said Anise. "What are we going to do now?"

"Burn," said Iggy sagely.

Anise didn't need Iggy's answer; she already knew her own. *What did you do when you were lost, unsure of yourself, and didn't know what to do next? You went home.*

HERO

1

T he horses raced up to the town gate. William, who was on guard duty this afternoon, hopped off his chair, ran over to the gate, and started trying to pull it closed. If he remembered it right, the protocol was that you were supposed to challenge people if they came in groups of more than two or three. It was harder to challenge people with the gates wide open.

"I'm getting too old for this," William muttered to himself as he struggled with the heavy wooden gate.

He was relieved when the riders stopped in front of the open gate rather than riding through. There were six of them. Five were men at arms in the blue tabards and chain mail of the king's guard. The other was a young blond woman. The tabards bore the black silhouette of a wolf's head that king Twilight had adopted as his symbol when he took the throne.

The five guardsmen stopped their horses smoothly, with the practiced skill of people who had been riding since they were young. The woman's horse took several extra steps as if she hadn't communicated the message to the animal well enough.

"Hello," she called out to William. She looked from left to right at the men riding with her as her horse continued to take mincing steps over the cobbles.

Several of the men dismounted smoothly and came over to her to help. One took her horse's head, and another helped her dismount. She sighed and sagged against the horse's side when she reached the ground. Then she straightened and knocked some of the dust from the road off her clothes.

William gave up on the gate and walked over to where they were.

"Can I help you?" he said. He tried to hide his

excitement. This was the most action he'd seen on gate duty in years.

The blond woman smiled at him. It was a sweet smile that immediately made him like her. "Sorry," she said. "I've just been learning to ride. I've gotten pretty good at the part where the horse just gallops on, following the other horses, but getting on and off is still a challenge. And, I get a lot more tired than they do." She glanced at the guardsmen.

She looked dressed in elegant finery to William, though her clothes were simple by court standards. Made of fine material, the cut of the blue tunic seemed customary. Still, the unusual thing about her outfit was her leggings. Aside from whether or not William had ever seen a woman in leggings at all, they were made of softened leather and seemed to have multiple pockets. There was a little road dust on her clothes, but it didn't detract from their grace.

She continued, "Anyway. What I'm here for is to deliver some news. Can you get the family of Anise, The Girl Who Dreamed, for me?"

2

The afternoon sun was a little warm. The blond woman and the five guardsmen moved into the shade under the gatehouse to wait. Though summery, it was a pleasant day. The village was quiet, at least where they were, and the wait was restful.

The quiet was interrupted by the rapid patter of bare feet on cobbles. A young girl came racing through the gate into the cobbled area outside it. She stopped immediately upon seeing the guardsmen and tried to act like she hadn't been running. Her charade was marred by her being out of breath.

The blond woman rose and stepped over to the girl. "Hail, and well met," she said.

The girl was just a little shorter than the woman, but, like her, she was blond. Her hair hung to her shoulders in gentle curls. Her hair color was lighter than the woman's. It was a yellow that almost looked white. She was dressed in a simple beige linen smock. Her eyes shone bright blue. She was just old enough to be somewhere between a girl and a young woman, though you couldn't tell it by how she was acting.

She breathed heavily, looked the woman up and down, and blurted out excitedly, "Are you the queen?" Then she looked down at the ground, crossed one leg in front of the other, and scraped her bare dirty big toe across the cobbles. "Sorry, your ladyship," she said.

The woman laughed. "Of course not. My name is Aela. I'm very pleased to meet you."

The girl remembered something. She executed a successful but clearly unfamiliar curtsy. "I'm Sunny," she said.

"You certainly are," said Aela. "Are you related to Anise?"

"You mean The Girl Who Dreamed?" said Sunny. "I think so. They tell me she's my aunt or cousin or something."

Aela scanned the girl again. In addition to the beige smock, she had a chain around her neck, with a shiny golden amulet hanging on it. It glinted in the afternoon sun. Aela recognized it as matching the medallion she had seen around Anise's neck.

A murmur of voices came through the gate, and a group of people walked out into the sunlight.

3

Three people walked into the cobbled square in front of the gatehouse. The bouncy young girl Aela had spoken with transformed in front of her eyes. Sunny straightened her back and moved up to the incoming trio. She nodded almost regally to Aela. "Aela," she said, "I'd like you to meet my Aunt Rose and my parents, Sebastian and Isabel." She turned to the three newcomers and nodded to them as well. Her words started speeding up as she continued, "Aunt Rose, Mama, and Papa, I'd like you to meet Aela. She has something to tell us about The Girl Who Dreamed."

The woman who Sunny had introduced as Isabel gazed at Sunny. "Thank you for that excellent introduction, Sunshine," she said and smiled.

The other two turned to Aela. "Greetings," said the man, while the woman said at the same time, urgently, "What can you tell us about Anise?"

"Thank you for coming to talk to me," said Aela. "Are you all of Anise's family, or are more coming?"

"This is everyone," said Sebastian. Aela glanced at him. He was dressed in plain yet comfortable-looking farmer's clothes, a bit worn but patched lovingly. Aela might have thought of him as old if she had met him before she came to start living at the King's Seat in Capitol. Now, though, she encountered people older than herself more often than not.

"I have mixed tidings," said Aela. "And, I am sad to say I feel somewhat responsible for both pieces of news."

"Please," said Rose, "We've been betwixt and between so long that any tidings will be welcome."

"Of course," said Aela, "I'm sorry. Well, the good tidings are that Anise is awake and seems to be of not completely unsound mind."

115

Again, simultaneously, Sebastian and Rose spoke. "Awake!" said Rose, and "And, the unfavorable?" said Sebastian.

"The unfavorable," continued Aela, "is that she's run away, and we can't find her."

4

At first, Anise stayed off the road and traveled through the trees, paralleling it. Then pushing through the bushes got annoyingly difficult, so she walked along the road, sneaking off into the underbrush when she saw anyone coming. Then even that became too much, and she walked along the side of the road, avoiding eye contact with other travelers.

While she fought her way through the woods, Iggy flew above her. Once she started walking along the road, it seemed he understood that it wouldn't help if he were seen. He faded into a wisp of smoke and settled on her shoulder. Anise noticed that she hardly felt his weight when he was in his smoke aspect.

She got some looks, though she wasn't sure if they were for her clothes or because she was a woman traveling alone. She dreaded the moment when someone would confront her for whatever reason, but she prepared herself mentally for it.

The road headed almost due south. For the moment, it was paralleling the Dragon River on the eastern side. Anise knew that Hero was in the southeastern corner of Liamec, and the Academy was in the northwest. She would have to travel through almost the entire kingdom to get home.

She pushed her helmet back on her head and carried her gloves to make herself look less conspicuous. She wasn't sure how well it worked. The helmet with the skull face was cunningly designed. It was almost as unobtrusive as a hat when the visor was up. Still, her clothes were unusual looking.

After an encounter with a farmer driving his cart north, who looked suspiciously like he was thinking about saying something to her, Anise was on the verge of reconsidering walking along the road. She was looking at the underbrush to see if it was any thinner here when a crossroads came into view around a bend in the way.

A man sat on a rock by the intersection, next to the marker stones which told the travel directions. He had the expectant air of someone who was waiting for something. Anise was trying to avoid attention, but he didn't look threatening, and she needed to read the stones to know which road she should take.

As she got a little closer to the man, she observed him. He looked very relaxed as he sat on his rock, though alert at the same time. She wondered how one combined being relaxed and alert, but he was doing it. He wore a worn traveler's cloak with a golden clasp holding the front together. A backpack was sitting on the ground at his feet, with a well-handled lute beside it.

Anise gasped when he turned to face her. It was Briac.

5

Briac looked older. A little grizzled, a little taller. He had filled out from a young man to an adult. It took him a moment to recognize her, then it was his turn to gasp. "Anise?" he said. Then, "Anise!" He jumped up, ran over to her, and squeezed her into an embrace that took away the little breath she had left.

Anise remembered the last time she had seen Briac. He had been walking away from her after they had shared their goodbye kiss. She had thought about the young, handsome bard often since then but hadn't imagined seeing him again in a place like this.

When she could breathe again, she said, "Briac, What are you doing here?"

He met her eyes and laughed. "What am I doing here? Last I knew, you were snoring your life away in a bed in the Academy infirmary." His face adopted a more thoughtful expression. "I visited you," he said. "I tried to wake you." He shook his head. "I even yelled at you to wake up, but you weren't having any of it."

"Sorry," said Anise.

"So, when did you wake up? Where are you going? Why are you by yourself? And where did you get that outfit?" Briac gazed admiringly at the black armor, boots, and helmet Anise wore.

Iggy faded into view on Anise's shoulder, hissed at Briac, and then diffused into smoke again.

Briac started. "What was that!" he exclaimed.

"Oh," said Anise. "That's just Iggy." She flapped her hand at the smoke trail on her shoulder. "Iggy, come out and say hi."

Iggy faded halfway into view. His head and upper body were visible, but his lower body was still smoke. He gazed at

Briac suspiciously. Briac reached out his hand toward Iggy. The fire imp's suspicious look grew more intense.

Anise shook her head at Briac. "You might want to give him a little time," she said. Briac dropped his hand to his side.

She saw the golden brooch that held Briac's cloak together. It was a tree branch crafted out of gold or gold gilded. Little bells attached to the bottom of the clasp tinkled when Briac moved. She remembered the similar bronze pin he had shown her when he visited her at the Academy.

"Gold," said Anise. "You've moved up in the world."

"You'd think so, wouldn't you," said Briac, glancing down at the golden pin himself. "Sometimes, it feels like the errands, lessons, and ranks never end. There's a long way to go after gold." He gazed at her curiously. "In fact, I'm here because I'm on an assignment right now."

6

Anise smiled at Briac. "So," she said. "What's your assignment?" She looked for the young man she had known in that face. Then she looked for the kiss they had shared, what felt like an eternity ago. She thought she saw both, but she wasn't sure.

"Well," said Briac, "One thing about bards, especially bards in the bardic council, is they don't say anything straightforwardly if they can say it in a more convoluted way."

Briac shook his head woefully. "They told me to meet Death's Daughter at the Brierstock Kreuzung. The first thing I had to do was find Brierstock. It's a little town not far from here." He waved down the road to the west. "Then I had to figure out what a Kreuzung was."

Anise waited expectantly. She was a little reluctant to tell Briac that she thought she knew who Death's Daughter was. At least not yet.

Briac continued, "It turns out that some of the families that settled Brierstock were from Almany. Kreuzung means crossroads in Almains." He glanced at the inscribed marker stones next to the rock he was sitting on. "So I'm waiting here for Death's Daughter. I had thought that she might be a woman who is dying or almost dead? But that was just a conjecture. I have no idea." He patted the knife on his belt. "I hope she's not something really scary."

Iggy faded from smoke into solidity and hopped off Anise's shoulder. Briac watched him carefully and somewhat warily. The fire imp walked over where Briac's pack and lute leaned against a rock. He waddled a little bit as he walked. Like a goose, he moved more freely when flying than when walking.

Briac gazed at Anise to see if he should do anything about what the fire imp was doing. She shook her head.

Iggy pointedly ignored Briac. He sniffed a few times at the backpack, then plucked a string on the lute with a talon. The sound of the lute string rang out clearly.

"What did they tell you you should do when you meet Death's Daughter?" said Anise.

7

Sebastian gave Aela a look. Though he looked like a small-town farmer, which she believed him to be, something about his manner made him seem like more. He carried himself like the people she had been dealing with in the King's Seat in Capitol, like a noble or a gentleman. There was a confidence there that seemed out of place.

"What do you mean, she's run off, and you can't find her?" he said. "Why would she run off?"

Aela shook her head. "I was there when she woke. I spoke to her. She seemed in her right head. She understood where she was and what had happened. I left her for just a moment to try to get the healers, and when we returned, she was gone."

"You left her alone?" said Rose.

"We had no idea that she might run away. In fact, we still don't know why she did. I was hoping you might have some idea," said Aela. "She definitely ran from something, though. We found the spot where she made her way through the wall around the Academy."

Sebastian turned away from the group toward the gate back into town.

"Where do you think you're going?" said Isabel.

"I've got to get ready," said Sebastian. "I've got to go find her."

Two more people walked through the gate. The mayor of Hero had gained a bit of weight in the last few years. He walked with a cane and leaned somewhat heavily on Lilith, the town's cunning woman, who walked at his side.

They were followed a moment later by William.

"What tidings," called out the mayor heartily. His voice didn't need a cane. "What news of our Girl Who Dreams?"

123

"You're not going anywhere," said Isabel to Sebastian, "Not until we've talked about this." Sebastian's face acquired a stubborn look.

"Anise is awake, and she's run away," said Rose to the mayor and Lilith.

8

Mr. Thatcher, the farrier, was leading Sebastian through the stables. Mr. Thatcher's son, Brian, had been running the business of late, but Mr. Thatcher said he was in charge when it came time to equip the Knight of Moon & Shadow with steeds. He wheezed a bit as he showed Sebastian the horses.

"How about that one?" asked Sebastian. He gestured toward one of the stalls. A young-looking horse was peering over the stall door at them.

"She's a three-year-old mare," said Mr. Thatcher. "She'd be a good choice for you. She's calm and social."

Sebastian reached over and rubbed the mare's neck. She pushed her head against his arm. She had an intelligent look in her eyes and a light, bright yellow coloring that reminded him of the color of Sunshine's hair. "What's her name?" said Sebastian.

"Most horses don't know their names; they mostly recognize their owner's voices," said Mr. Thatcher. "Why don't you come up with what you want to call her."

"Hay-bale," said Sebastian immediately.

"Why can't I come with you?" pouted Sunny.

"We've been over this, Sunshine," said Sebastian. They were in their barn. Sebastian was grooming Hay-bale with a curry comb. "It could be dangerous, and I don't know how long I'll be gone. And, if I even thought about letting you come, I'd have to find myself a new wife."

"But, I could be helpful," said Sunny. "You've been teaching me how to sword fight, and you said I have eyes in the back of my head."

Sebastian turned and looked his daughter in the eye.

125

"I'm sure you would be, Sunny, but I'm afraid it won't happen."

Aela and her guardsmen left the village. As they prepared to ride out the gate, Aela pressed something like a coin into Sebastian's hand.

"What's this?" he asked.

"It's a King's Favor," said Aela. Sebastian studied the token in his hand. It had an engraving of a wolf's head on one side and on the other a tower. Aela continued, "It's a symbol that you have some connection to someone close to the king. It might be useful in your search." She smiled at him. "Come to the King's Seat, and show it to the guards. I'll notify them to admit you. You can check to see if we've had any luck in our own search."

9

Lilith insisted on giving Sebastian potions and magical aid on his journey. Her one regret from when he had traveled as the Knight of Moon & Shadow was that she hadn't been ready to provide him with more help. Though, at the time, she had felt a little outclassed by the magic he had been bearing.

She gave him her signaling potion. The same one he had used when he brought Anise home from the Academy one summer. This time, she told him that if he released the catch, mixed the yellow and blue fluids, and signaled her, she would take it to mean that he had found Anise, and she would tell Rose and Isabel.

She gave him several potions that promoted healing and increased strength. There were a few others as well. She instructed him what each one did and when to use it. Then they packed them carefully into one of Hay-bale's saddlebags. Sebastian had the mental image of opening the saddlebag and finding nothing but a stew of frothing fluids and broken glass. Still, they were wrapped and padded so thoroughly that, hopefully, that wouldn't happen.

The mayor planned a big farewell gathering for Sebastian's departure. He might be having trouble walking without his cane, but that didn't mean that city affairs were any less important. Sebastian derailed the effort by sneaking out of the village at night with just a goodbye kiss for his wife and daughter.

Sebastian sat by his campfire. He had found a good spot for it inside one of the circles of stones found near the roads and by-ways of Liamec. Hay-bale was tethered on the other side of the firepit. He had tied her so she had enough lead to graze but couldn't go too far.

"It's a beautiful night, isn't it, girl?" he said.

She nodded. Though, some might have thought she was just lifting and lowering her head as she grazed.

Sebastian was enjoying his first night of camping since leaving Hero. It was cold, and there were hardships, but it reminded him of other times, which wasn't totally amiss.

"It's too bad you never got to meet Betsy," Sebastian said. "You would have liked her."

Hay-bale lifted her head, met Sebastian's eyes, and nickered.

"She would have liked you too," he said. He hesitated, then continued reluctantly, "Well, she probably wouldn't have liked you, but she might have tolerated you, for my sake."

10

Briac gazed at Anise curiously. "Why would you wonder what I'm supposed to do when I meet Death's Daughter before you wonder who she might be?" he said. He shook his head again. "Anyway," he continued, "what they told me to do was to escort Death's Daughter to her destination."

"I think I might be Death's Daughter," said Anise. "That's what they might be calling me, anyway."

Iggy kept staring at Briac's lute. He seemed to be fascinated by it.

"Why would anyone call you that?" asked Briac.

Anise reached up and flipped down the visor on her helmet. She pulled her spear from its sheath and summoned her shield from wherever it was when she didn't need it. Briac gasped.

"All right," he said. "I see it. Christ's ear lobes, that's scary. Please take that mask off."

Anise flipped the visor back up. The shield disappeared with a thought.

"Where did they tell you to take Death's Daughter? What's my destination?" asked Anise.

"What happened to you, Anise?" asked Briac. "We all thought you were just sleeping, but it seems like something happened, didn't it?"

Anise frowned. "I think my question is more urgent," she said.

Briac looked thoughtful. "All right," he said, "I wish I had a better answer for you. I wasn't told a destination. They just told me to escort Death's Daughter, you, to your destination. Damnable bards. Never a straight answer to a question."

"Aren't you a bard?" said Anise.

"That doesn't mean I can't curse the rest of them."

"Well, if you and the bards aren't going to provide me with a destination, I'll have to just stick to the one I was already heading for," said Anise.

"Where was that?" asked Briac.

"I was going to go home. I would like to go back to Hero to see my uncle and aunts."

Briac smiled. "That's fine. I've always wanted to see Hero. It's supposed to be a special town," he said.

"It is?" asked Anise. "What's supposed to be special about it?"

"Well," said Briac, "you and your uncle come from there, don't you?"

11

Briac and Anise set up camp for the evening. Briac had all the things Anise had been missing in his backpack. A pot for cooking, utensils, two cups, a waterskin, and some spices. He even had a little packet that he proudly showed her containing some salt.

They set up away from the road to avoid curious or prying eyes. Briac started getting used to Iggy flapping around and quickly appreciated his firewood gathering prowess. Once they had a fire going, Briac started adding ingredients for a traveler's soup. He had some leftover rabbit meat from a successful hunt the day before. Briac had become a decent shot with a sling and had had some luck with it.

Anise added what little she had gathered during the day. She was greatly looking forward to eating something more substantial than roots and berries. The smell of the simmering soup pot was making her water at the mouth.

Briac turned to her from where he was tending the soup to make sure it didn't overcook. He reached into his backpack and pulled out something else.

"Hey, Anise," he said, "Remember this?" He held it up in the air. It was a single withered turnip. "I bought it back at the market at Brierstock. I wasn't sure why." He flourished it over the pot before dropping it in. "For the soup," he said.

Later, after they had eaten and the stars were trying to peek through the graying sky, Anise asked, "Did the bards say anything else useful?"

"Well," said Briac, "I suppose that depends on what you think is useful."

"Was there more in this prophecy about Death's Daughter?"

"There was," said Briac thoughtfully. "It didn't make much sense to me at the time. I'm not sure if it makes any more sense now that I know that you're Death's Daughter." He placed his fingertips together with his fingers arched. His face acquired a slightly emotionless expression, and he started to intone the words of the prophecy. Anise guessed that this was how a bard recited a spoken piece.

"The byways of the soothsayers have gouged cracks through Dream and into reality. Existence will fracture, and the waking world will fall into ruin if Death's Daughter is not there to hold the pieces together." Briac took a breath and continued. "The storms will shatter the planes into fragments until all that remains is Death and Dream."

He relaxed his pose and smiled at Anise. It was a bit of a crooked smile. "It's all a bit depressing if you ask me."

Briac only had one bedroll. He kept it lashed to the bottom of his pack. It was getting toward the end of summer, and though the days were still warm, the evenings were getting cold. They spent the evening reminiscing about times past. Briac filled in Anise as much as he could about what had happened in Liamec while she was asleep. When they said all there was to say, there was an awkward moment where they both stared at the bedroll.

"I'll just sleep over there by the fire," said Briac.

"Don't be silly," said Anise. "It's your bedroll."

In the end, a compromise was reached where they both squeezed as best they could into the bedroll with Anise's spear between them.

THE KING'S SEAT

1

The first dream storm hit the land of Liamec that night. It was a little one, just a foreshadowing of things to come. Most of the kingdom was asleep. Only the night owls, moonlight thieves, and insomniacs were stirring.

Both Anise and Briac slept through it, though Anise stirred fitfully and restlessly.

Vix woke and put out her hand to make sure her husband, the king, was still sleeping soundly beside her.

Hay-bale nickered fearfully but not loudly enough to wake Sebastian.

Near the Academy and the town of Ashton, there was a cracking and crackling sound, which the night-pads and other moonlight dwellers who were awake and busy at their work heard. It didn't seem to come from anywhere in particular but rather from everywhere at once. The thieves paused, waited a moment to see if the sound had any meaning for them, and then went about their business.

The people most affected by that first storm, the ones who would remember it, were those who had gotten up to get a sip of water or use the privy. Walking through a darkened house or a dim yard, with nothing but a flickering candle flame or perhaps a trace of moonlight to light their way, they already were prone to glimpse things out of the corners of their eyes. They would always look to see if the thing seen was really there. The confirmation that it was just a shadow or a trick of the light, or lack of light, brought back the comfort of the distance between reality and dream.

That night, that storm, that moment, brought something different. When those moonlight candlelight walkers turned and looked to see if their imagination was playing tricks on them, for a moment, they saw whatever nightmare or bad dream they had known was there.

Just for a moment, for each of them, that nightmare *was* there.

2

Briac and Anise were standing on a grassy hillside looking out at the city walls of Capitol, and beyond them, the towers, spires, and battlements of the castle called the King's Seat. "I'd like to see it," said Anise. The keeps, walls, and fortifications of the Seat stretched to the horizon beyond the city walls.

"We are seeing it," said Briac with a smile.

"It's just," said Anise, "You hear so much about Capitol, the King's Seat, and the court. I never thought I would ever see it. Now, though, I feel like I will."

"Of course you will," said Briac. "We could go down now and try to get past the guards at the gate?"

"No," Anise shivered, though the morning sun was warm. "I want to find some friends, some family. I don't know what Lorenzo is up to or how far his reach extends."

"You have some friends," said Briac. "Or, at least one." He reached out his hand and rested it on her shoulder. The black material of her armor felt tough yet pliable under his hand.

"Of course," said Anise, "Sorry." Iggy faded into view on her shoulder. His hissing at Briac had gotten a little quieter, but that was his only concession to friendliness so far.

They found a spot to camp that evening where they felt comfortable lighting a fire. It was wooded enough that the light wouldn't show very far, and they tried to keep the smoke down.

After they had eaten, Briac brought out his lute and started tuning the strings. It was the first time he had played since they had met at the crossroads outside Brierstock. Iggy, relaxing in the campfire, lifted his head and stared fixedly at the lute.

"Play me something," said Anise.

Briac smiled at her. "Not a problem," he said.

He started into the instrumental part of a song. The notes floated through the air like moths above the campfire flames. Anise felt like she could see them.

Iggy leaned back into the burning brands and coals of the fire, his eyes lost focus, and he started making a noise that sounded like a cat purring. "Burn," he said languidly.

3

The moon shone down on the Lion's tawny mane.
He stalked the night through the wind and icy rain.
He'd left his Seat, his lair, perched high on its hill,
to hunt the night for the thrill of the kill.

A wolf cub, weak and small, young, newly born,
stood in a clearing, exposed, alone, forlorn,
The Lion saw his meal; he sensed his prey,
but after the fray, it was he who lost his way.

For the cub, not yet fully grown,
was Twilight, the young king coming to his own.
The Lion's dream of victory, a kingdom in thrall,
was soon to fail, and all would see his fall.

The cub was young, but he was the true heir,
And with his friends, the Fox, Falcon, and Bear,
He fought until the Lion was laid low.
The beast fell; the final blow brought his woe.

With the battle won, the Lion's hope was gone,
He'd shown his weakness, the wolf his brawn,
Those watching, those in Liamec far and near,
saw the wolf, our new king, without peer or fear.

4

Briac and Anise walked down the road away from Capitol and the King's Seat. Iggy was just a trace of smoke on Anise's shoulder. Since listening to Briac play, he had stopped hissing at him. Instead, he just stared at the bard with a confused expression.

"You remember Drun Coeloc," said Briac.

"Of course," said Anise, "The bard who left the bardic order and became a master at the Academy. You read his papers."

"Yes," said Briac, "well, a couple of years ago, the master scribe of the council found a damaged journal of master Coeloc's from his time after he left the Academy. He returned to the bards and lived the remainder of his days in Taliesin. The scribe knew I had looked into Drun's past at the Academy, and he showed the journal to me."

"What did it say?" said Anise curiously.

"Well, you know how the dragons are coming back?" asked Briac.

"They are?"

Briac frowned. "I thought I told you about that. Ashton has been attacked several times. There have been numerous sightings in the northwest of Liamec."

Anise remembered looking back at Ashton as she was leaving and seeing the scaffolding on the Dragon Watchtower. Now it was clear why it was being rebuilt.

Briac continued, "I mentioned that because the journal pages told how Coeloc knew something about dragons. Apparently, the bards got along with them better than the Academy ever managed to. Coeloc himself said he could talk to them. He called himself a Dragon Speaker. He said that he had gotten his calling to go to the Academy and get them to stop studying clairvoyance from something he'd heard from a dragon."

Anise got excited. "That's what I told master Huginn," she said.

"Anyway," said Briac, "I just thought you'd find that interesting."

5

Hay-bale whinnied nervously as Sebastian led her into the line of people awaiting entrance to the King's Seat. There was a small group of guardsmen in the blue tabards of the king's men asking questions of people trying to enter. Most people were either admitted to the castle or turned away quickly, so the line moved swiftly.

Hay-bale was a small-town horse. She wasn't used to big cities. The walls loomed overhead, and the other horses and numerous people made her nervous. Sebastian patted her on the neck to try to calm her.

While they waited, Sebastian checked out the walls and what they saw through the gates. He was from the same small town as Hay-bale and understood her nerves.

The King's Seat was the biggest castle Sebastian had ever seen. It was larger than any castle he could even imagine. The Young Lion, the prince regent who King Twilight had deposed, had devoted the construction efforts of Liamec for years to expanding and enhancing the hereditary seat of the Kings of Liamec. Like the Egyptian Pharaohs, he had wanted his legacy to live on after him.

The Seat sprawled, rambled, and stretched its way throughout the capital city of Liamec, Capitol. It had grown until it was larger than many towns in the country. The Seat's outer walls met with the city's exterior walls in places. If the Prince Regent had succeeded in his efforts to become king, he might have expanded the Seat until it reached the city walls all around. Then the Seat and the city might have become synonymous.

Sebastian felt a little teary-eyed. He remembered when he had first started hearing the stories about the new king, Twilight, and how he had unseated the cruel prince regent. It had hurt that this new young king, so healthy and mighty, had the same name as his innocent long-dead son. He and Isabel had never spoken of it, but he thought he had seen the same hurt in her eyes.

Sebastian reached the front of the line. He wore the purple jacket, thick white dyed linen britches, and black boots that Isabel and Anise had made him long ago. The thistledown that stuffed the quilted pockets of the jacket had gotten a little crushed, but it was still warm and tough. He had thought about leaving Hero without the outfit, but it had felt wrong to go on a quest without his armor. So, he had pulled the clothes out of their closet, dusted them off, and now felt like a proper fool as the guardsmen looked him over.

The guardsmen laughed. One of them turned to the others and said, "Look at this one. He thinks he's the Knight of Moon & Shadow."

Sebastian stepped forward, held Hay-bale's lead tightly so she wouldn't shy, and pulled the token Aela had given him out of his belt pouch.

6

Sebastian walked down the red carpet that led from the large double doors of the king's vast throne room toward the raised dais where the throne stood. The throne was partially hidden behind the king and his group of advisers. Sebastian was being escorted by one of the king's guardsmen.

The hall was wide and long, though it was longer than it was wide. Both sides were lined with high windows and crowds of people present for the day's court proceedings. Sebastian could hear some of them murmuring about him. His clothing and the road dust covering him were drawing attention.

The late morning sunlight flooded into the room through the windows on one side. Behind the dais that the throne and the king's retinue stood on were several tall stained glass windows depicting scenes from the history of Liamec.

The guardsman halted at the dais's foot and gestured for Sebastian to do the same. There was a little bit of whispering between some of the king's attendants, and one of them stepped forward. In a voice that was clearly intended to, and trained to, fill the room, he called out, "Sebastian of Hero, with a petition for the king!"

A young man stepped forward from the crowd in front of the throne. Though he wore no crown and was dressed in fine but unpretentious clothes, Sebastian thought he must be the king by his bearing. He walked a few steps down the dais and asked Sebastian, "How can I help you, friend?"

Sebastian performed a half bow. He surprised himself with his graceful execution of the move. A half-memory of his father and mother drilling him in things like that came to mind. He'd never had a call to use the knowledge before.

"Your Majesty," he said. "I am seeking the one who has

become known as The Girl Who Dreamed. She's my niece. The Lady Aela advised me to ask here if there had been any word, or news, of her."

"Of course," said the young king sympathetically, "both my queen and the lady Aela have been talking of nothing else." He shook his head. "I'm afraid we have no new tidings."

Sebastian assessed the young king in front of him. For a moment, buried grief surfaced. This young man, strong and handsome, was just about the same age his own son, Twilight, would have been if he had lived.

The king continued. "This search for your missing relative strikes me as a noble quest. I will help you in whatever way I can. Can I provide you with some guardsmen to accompany you and help you on your journey?"

Sebastian met the young king's eyes. "Your majesty," he said, "I wouldn't know what to do with guardsmen. I am not a leader of men, and I am used to traveling alone. I merely hoped that there might be some word or news. The Lady Aela was very helpful when she visited us in Hero."

"Of course," said the king. "I am sorry that we don't have any tidings. I would like to provide you with supplies and other equipment to help you on your way." He focused on the man in the blue tabard standing next to Sebastian. "Guardsman," he said, "Please escort our guest to Smithy and see that he is provided with everything he needs."

7

Smithy was a big man. He greeted Sebastian with a hearty laugh. "There's something special about you, my good man," he said. "I've got orders from the king to treat you almost like you were one of the family."

They were standing in the Smith's Yard. Sebastian's guardian guardsman had led him here. The clatter of hammers and the creaking of bellows from all the various forges made a mighty din. It didn't seem to make a difference to Smithy's voice. He spoke strongly enough that he could be heard even over the clamor.

"What that mostly means is this," the smith continued. His sooty leather smith's apron was worn with use. He held out a silvery piece of fabric. With his big meaty hands, he spread it out. It was a tunic made of some shiny material. The way the big smith held it made it look almost weightless.

"What is that?" said Sebastian.

"It's armor," said the smith. "We call it attercop armor. It's something special that the queen and I work on. Like I said, you're unusual." He shook the tunic a little. It shimmered in the sunlight that was slanting into the yard. "It's lightweight, and yet it can stop a longbow arrow. Put it on." He handed the metal shirt to Sebastian.

The shirt was light. The material slid smoothly over Sebastian's hands. He pulled and prodded at it a little. It seemed to be all that Smithy had said it was. He removed his purple thistledown jerkin and put the tunic on.

Smithy took in Sebastian's faded jacket as he started putting it back on over the lightweight chain mail. "Would you like a nice new leather jerkin to replace that?" he asked.

Sebastian shook his head. "No, thank you," he said. "this has sentimental value for me."

Smithy inspected Sebastian when he was done putting the shirt on. "Do you need a weapon?" he asked. He focused on Sebastian's sword, which had been returned to him as he left the throne room.

Sebastian pulled the weapon partway out of its sheath. "I'm all right," he said, "I've got my father's sword."

The brawny smith stared at the blade and hilt in Sebastian's hand. "Wait a minute," he said, "I recognize that. Isn't that …"

Sebastian thrust the sword back into the sheath. "It's my father's sword, and that's all it is," he said.

"Oh, yes. Of course it is," said the smith. He glanced up and met Sebastian's eyes with a smile.

8

A nise sat quietly by the fire, cross-legged. Briac was out searching for more firewood. She had given him strict orders not to disturb her when he returned. He had told her that the Academy had been graduating clairvoyants at a pretty good rate. They had been doing so for the last ten years.

As part of the class's research in Anise's clairvoyance class, they learned theoretical techniques. However, they hadn't done any practical work. Anise thought that if there was ever a time when it would be helpful to know the truth or get a glimpse of the future, it would be now.

They were a little far from the Academy for Anise's taste. One of the things they had learned in class and that Briac had confirmed was that, unlike the other disciplines, clairvoyance was more potent the closer you were to the Academy. Briac told her that most of the graduating clairvoyants settled in Ashton, Lakeside, or nearby towns.

The process, which Anise had learned theoretically, was in several steps. The first was entering a meditative trance. Anise had started working on that as soon as Briac left the firepit they had set up for the evening. The next step was establishing a mental connection to the staging area, or the Room of Doors, as the references from her class had called it. To Anise's understanding, this was a place that was almost like a dream that the clairvoyants shared in common.

You entered the room of doors, and there was debate whether this was through a dream or astral projection. Then you picked your door and followed the path behind it. What happened next was different depending on who the clairvoyant was and which pathway they traveled.

The little Anise had been able to read about the paths

was confusing. One clairvoyant had described traveling down the Path of Flowers when clients asked her about their wedding. She spoke about looking through seas of roses, violets, and other blossoms, looking for a glimpse of a groom or a bride.

Another told of traveling the Path of Death when he tried to find out how long someone had to live. That story hadn't ended well, with the clairvoyant ending the journey early in fear for their own life.

Anise focused on her breathing and her thoughts. Finding the room of doors felt like a different thing than entering into a channeling dream. Some images came from her subconscious mind when she entered a channeling dream. In this case, she was trying to find a shared creation, something that was in some ways more real, perhaps, than the realms visited in dreams.

Anise had tried to connect to the room of doors several times during her clairvoyance class without success. This time, even with the Academy as distant as it was, it felt easier.

Anise felt herself stepping into a huge chamber filled with doors of every shape and size.

9

The room of doors was vast. There were archways, entryways, openings, and doorways on every side. There were even hatchways and trapdoors on the floor. Some of the doors were dust-covered and looked like they hadn't been accessed in eons; others appeared like someone might have stepped through them just moments ago. The stone walls looked worn and ancient. The ceiling, somewhere high above, was an indeterminate gray color. Anise wasn't sure if there was a ceiling or the gray was swirling fog.

There was no one but Anise there. It came to her that perhaps it was easier for her to access this place now because it was being used more. Maybe the clairvoyants from the Academy were beating a path through the realms to these doors.

The center of the room was taken up by a large fixed stone basin. The stone bowl looked as ancient as the walls and floor. It might be a pool or bath, but it was sealed with a locked iron cover.

She thought about how she was going to choose which door to open. They all looked different. Each had its own unique character. A large black door set in a heavy frame near her had a skull engraved into its surface. Looking at it, Anise felt a shiver that reminded her of how she had felt the first time she saw Lord Hades. She thought she knew how the paths got their names. This door had to lead to the Path of Death.

Anise thought. What did she want to know? She wanted to know where to go next, how to stop Lorenzo, and how to save the world. She inspected the nearby doors.

Some pathway portals were easy to recognize. Anise saw the Path of Life with green curling plant fronds almost obscuring the entranceway. Some were more difficult. A small barred hatchway chained and padlocked gave her a deep feeling of mystery.

Anise wandered for a bit through the chamber, looking at the doors. She saw the Door of Truth. It was a blue door with daffodils carved into the wooden frame. The stylized head of an owl adorned the center. One of her texts had described the daffodils, owl's head, and blue color. It looked heavily traveled.

The truth was what she was looking for, wasn't it? Maybe this was the door she should open.

Anise's gaze was caught by another door. It was a massive steel construction with a sculpted dragon's head built into the top of the frame. The eyes, glowing like rubies, cut angrily into her heart. Almost involuntarily, she walked over to it and reached out for the handle, shaped like a dragon's claw.

10

A nise opened the door. The iron dragon's claw handle felt cold in her hand. The door swung open with a creak and thudded against the stone wall. It was easier to open than it should have been for such a massive piece of metal. She stepped through the door frame.

Anise was confused and couldn't understand what she was looking at. There was a gravel path on the ground leading away from the door frame, but there was no stone wall around it on the other side of the doorway. The door frame stood by itself, rising from the ground.

The pathway led into a mist that reminded Anise of the fog surrounding the Isle of the Wise. In fact, it felt like that same mist. Anise was almost disappointed. She had been expecting something more dramatic. Perhaps the other paths were different? She took a step out onto the pathway and away from the door.

As soon as Anise put her feet on the gravel, she felt the pathway draw her feet down it. It wasn't like she was walking down a path, but more like sliding along a grooved track. The mist continued on both sides. Without knowing how she knew it, she knew that she wouldn't be able to step off the way.

The path started to curve around a bend, and Anise thought she saw a little clearing of the mist ahead. Some color was leaching into the world, and she would be able to see something other than gray fog.

A sound broke through the stillness, the beating of heavy wings. Even though the mist obscured the light, so there was no apparent source, a shadow cast itself over the path ahead of Anise. A massive creature landed with a thud on the track before her.

It was Flambé, the dragon. Her black scaly face turned to

Anise; she opened her mouth and roared. A thought intruded into Anise's mind. *Your kind are not welcome here.*

I want to help, thought Anise. *I can do something to help if you trust me. If you let me in.*

Trust? You? Came the thought. *Your kind are nothing but betrayal and ill faith. Look at what he is doing. He has found his way to the Keep and is searching for the keys to the Scrying Pool.*

Who? thought Anise. *The Keep? The Scrying Pool?*

Your clairvoyants, they don't know what they are doing! These aren't paths; they are cracks in the fabric separating reality from dream. Every time a clairvoyant walks a track, they gouge the fracture deeper. And now, with the dark one trying to open the Scrying Pool, it will just worsen.

I will talk no more. Your wards may keep us from stopping your kind from using the other paths, the other cracks, but this one leads out of your territory. This one leads to our home. This one I can protect.

The dragon reared back and loosed a blast of fiery breath at Anise. The flames washed over her. She felt the heat and the pressure of the dragon's breath. She felt her spirit forced off the path and back into her meditating body.

When she opened her eyes, Iggy flapped in the air above her. He waved his talons excitedly above her head. "Burn," he exclaimed.

11

Hay-bale was enormously relieved to be riding away from the gates of Capitol. She was a small-town horse. The ways of the big city were not for her. Sebastian reached out and stroked her neck. "How was it in those crowded stables?" he asked.

Hay-bale nickered. Perhaps she was responding to his question. Maybe she was complaining about the additional weight in her saddlebags from the supplies the king's guardsmen had loaded into them.

Sebastian shifted in the saddle. He felt the presence of the extra layer of armor on his shoulders, though he hardly felt the weight. The additional armor felt good, however. When he was younger, he had felt invincible on his quest as the Knight of Moon & Shadow. He hadn't worried about whether or not something would happen to him. Now, he just wanted to make sure that he made it back to Isabel and Sunshine safely.

"Where are we going to go next?" he asked. The question stumped Hay-bale.

With Hay-bale not providing any answers, Sebastian thought about the question himself. He realized why Isabel might have thought him ill-advised to venture forth on this quest. As the Knight of Moon & Shadow, he'd had supernatural guidance. Luna had been with him every step of the way. Liamec might be a small land by most standards, but it was a pretty extensive territory for one man and one horse to search for one missing person.

Well, he thought, *where do I start looking when I lose something at home?*

The answer was obvious; you started looking in the last

place you had the thing you lost.

They needed to go to the Academy.

12

The second dream storm struck in the early evening. Unlike the first storm, this one happened when most of the land of Liamec was awake. The cracking sound that preceded the disturbance was louder this time. For those near Ashton, the first crack was an almost deafening boom.

People's dreams came to life.

Briac was out gathering firewood. The last traces of the setting sun still lit the sky, making it that part of an evening where the lighting was called twilight. He heard the barrage of the nascent storm. He dropped the wood he was carrying. The initial booming crack was replaced by a crackling sound.

Briac looked around himself, trying to see if he could see anything that could cause such a sound. Then he started through the trees back towards where he and Anise had set up camp. She might still be meditating and could be vulnerable.

There was a rustling in the gray shadows in the underbrush on both sides of Briac. He wasn't sure at first what was making the noise. Then he knew or thought he knew, though he didn't know how he knew.

It was spiders. Lots of spiders. Briac shivered; he'd never liked spiders. He started to run. The gray lighting made it hard to see his footing. The rustling sound grew louder, then louder still. He scrambled his way through the underbrush.

Briac tripped, or perhaps something tripped him. He stumbled and fell. The brush near him started stirring. Multiple hairy legs thrust themselves out of the foliage. Briac gasped and crawled back, away from the wall of leaves.

A spider came scuttling out of the bush. It leered at Briac, making a chittering noise. Where arachnid features should have been was a human face. It started advancing toward where Briac was lying awkwardly on the ground. Its face was the face of his master in the council of Bards. A scowl of deep disapproval was manifest on that face.

The crackling that had pervaded the background sounds slowed and stopped. Briac blinked, rubbed his eyes, and the spider was gone.

Those who were asleep were lucky if they were between dreams. Some of the people who were having very bad dreams didn't wake up. Some of the people who were having very good dreams didn't want to wake up.

Those who were awake had run-ins with their dreams. Brief. Brief enough to survive for most of those who encountered their nightmares.

GRISPUT

1

Anise woke slowly in the morning. Her trials with clairvoyance had worn her out. Briac was leaning over the campfire cooking the last of the eggs he had bought at the Brierstock market. "Should we talk about what happened last night?" he said.

"What happened last night?" asked Anise.

Briac put the pot with the eggs onto a boulder by the edge of the firepit and handed Anise a wooden spoon. "The crackling, crunching noises, and the spiders." He shivered.

Anise shook her head. "I'm not sure what you're talking about."

Briac frowned. "Maybe you were still meditating," he said slowly.

Later, after they had walked for most of the day, Briac started checking the oncoming travelers carefully as soon as they came into sight.

"We have to take a little care for the next bit," he said. "We don't want to run into the Grisput guards."

"Can't we just avoid the city?" said Anise.

"We'd have to go quite a bit out of our way to avoid it completely," said Briac. "The main road runs right through Grisput, and there aren't too many other choices." He frowned. "We should be all right if we're just a bit careful."

It was Anise's turn to frown when they were crouching in the brush off the side of the road, watching a troop of guardsmen marching by. They were wearing purple tabards with a black silhouette of a coiled serpent on the front. "I don't like this," she said. "We shouldn't have to hide."

"Better to be safe than sorry," said Briac, "We don't want to run afoul of the guard."

"What could they do?" said Anise, "We haven't done

anything wrong."

"That doesn't really matter to them," said Briac, "they don't need much excuse. They're always looking for new bondsmen and women to sell at the bond market."

"They'd sell us?" asked Anise indignantly. Iggy hissed on her shoulder. "They can't do that! That's not right."

Briac just shook his head sadly. He held a finger in front of his lips and glanced through the underbrush at the marching troop.

2

Sebastian was riding Hay-bale into the town of Brierstock. Brierstock was mainly known for its market. The settlers of Brierstock were from Almany, and they were famous for their woodworking and craftsmanship. The market also sold food and other goods. It was open every day except sun's day.

They rode into the marketplace. The market, bustling each of the other times Sebastian had passed through town, was quiet, and many of the booths were shuttered. Hay-bale looked disappointed. She had been anticipating a treat.

Sebastian called out to a man walking through the mostly empty marketplace, "Why are all the shops and carts shuttered?"

"The dreams from yesterday," the man answered, "Everyone's trying to recover."

"The dreams?" said Sebastian.

The man stared at Sebastian. The expression on his face made Sebastian think of how one might look at a slow child.

"Yesterday, when all our dreams came to life," he said, "Everyone felt it."

Sebastian shook his head. The man stared for a second in disbelief, then walked on.

They rode on a bit through the empty streets. The sun was shining on the cobbles of the road. Hay-bale was in a good mood and listened attentively to Sebastian's musings.

"You know," he said, "I did have something like a dream coming to life yesterday." Hay-bale nickered encouragingly. "Remember?" he continued. "I was almost falling asleep in the saddle, there was that strange sound, and then I felt like I was talking to Isabel and Sunshine?" He pressed his finger to his lips thoughtfully. "It felt like they were really there." He shook his head. "Why would everyone be upset about something like that?"

3

Sebastian tied Hay-bale to a hitching post outside a pub with Der Bunte Hund written on the sign. Above the words was a wooden dog with faded rainbow-colored paint on it. The dog stood unsteadily on its back legs and held an ale mug in its forepaws. Hay-bale gave Sebastian a resentful look as he finished with the reins.

"I know," he said, "But I don't think you'd be welcome inside."

Inside it was small and close, with wooden beams hanging low overhead. It reminded Sebastian of the pub back in Hero. Sebastian didn't spend too much time there, but he did stop in every now and then. He took a seat at the bar and flagged down the pub-keeper for an ale.

As he usually did when he went to the pub in Hero, Sebastian sat on his barstool and looked around the pub's interior. He found that listening and keeping quiet was often an excellent way to learn.

Several conversations were going on. Though the streets outside were empty, many of the people who weren't out there were here.

Two men sitting near Sebastian discussed what had happened with their dreams the day before.

One of them had been chased through the village streets by some mysterious unseen figure, and the other had been trapped in his own home, unable to get out. The second man had opened door after door, trying to exit his home, only to find them leading to unfamiliar rooms. The mysterious unseen figure the first one had seen had chased him for the duration of the dream time, vanishing just as he fled down a dark alley that ended in a dead-end.

Sebastian switched his attention to the conversation on the other side of himself. These people were discussing someone called "Death's Daughter."

"I saw her," said one of them to the other. "Just a little north of here. Before everyone was talking about her."

His companion made appropriately interested noises, and the first man continued, "It was after the Scute Bridge. You know, the one that crosses over the Dragon River toward Ashton. I was on my way to Meara with my crop of cabbage."

The second man frowned. "You've got to stop going up there. Sooner or later, they're just going to cut your throat and rob you. They're pirates; they can't be trusted."

"They pay really well for my cabbages," the first one continued, "Apparently, it's good for sea voyages. Stops some kind of disease." He shook his head, "Anyway, I saw Death's Daughter like I was saying. She had a face like a skull. She was fighting against a strange creature." He shivered. "It was a nightmare. I practically pissed myself looking at it. It looked like a bad dream."

4

Anise was sound asleep. She felt a presence intrude itself into her slumber. "Anise, dear," said a quiet, calm woman's voice, "I think it would be a good idea for you to wake up now." She opened her eyes to see moonlight streaming into the clearing where she and Briac were sleeping. It shone down onto their bedroll and the embers of the fire they had laid the night before.

Her medallion felt warm on her chest. She sat up and started quietly fastening the clasps on her armor. Briac snuffled a slight snore into the night air.

Iggy stirred as well. He looked up at Anise from where he lay beside the bedroll. In the beginning, Iggy tried to sleep next to her under the blanket. But, he generated too much heat, and she kicked him out. He still slept as close to her as he could. The feeling of his small body pressed against hers, even from outside the bedroll, was reassuring.

Anise heard some scuffling sounds under the trees outside the clearing in the brush. She stood, pulled on her gloves, put her helmet on her head, and took her spear into her right hand. There was a trace of torchlight glimmering through the trees.

Anise dropped the visor of her helmet over her face. "Who's there?" she called out. The helmet deepened and changed her voice. Iggy flapped his wings and took up a position over her head. Briac started and sat upright, wiping the sleep out of his eyes.

Four men charged into the clearing. They were dressed in the purple tabards and chain mail Anise had seen earlier. Another one stepped in a little after the first four. "Submit to the Grisput guard," he called out, "You're under arrest for vagrancy."

Briac scrambled to his feet, feeling around the bedroll for his knife. Iggy flapped his wings menacingly at the men and hissed.

Anise lifted her arms, shield on one, spear held in the other. She felt the moonlight on her face, even through the visor of her helmet. She knew that the skull contour was glowing with the luminescence of the heavenly body. "You've picked the wrong victims this night," she bellowed.

Anise disregarded the shield on one arm, and the spear clutched in her other hand. She brought her arms together in a sweeping motion and conjured a surge of wind toward the men. Iggy flapped desperately to stay in the air, even though he was out of the main path of the windstorm. All five men were blown backward towards the trees, their weapons and shields clattering to the earth.

From the ground, one of the men sputtered, "Death's Daughter ... ." Three of them took off running through the underbrush, leaving their equipment lying there. The leader and the one who had spoken started reaching to pick up their weapons.

Iggy swooped forward and blasted the area with his fiery breath. The remaining men abandoned their gear and took off after their companions.

5

Briac and Anise were talking while breaking their fast. Breakfast this morning was some hard bread and cheese. Anise had thought about warming her cheese in the fire-pit embers, like her uncle used to, but decided it was too much work. Instead, she was chewing on the hard cheese and regretting her decision.

Briac had suggested that they move on in case the guards came back, but Anise had gotten a look on her face and just said, "Let them come." Briac had never seen a look like that on Anise's face before. He wasn't sure what to make of it.

"Once we're the rest of the way past Grisput," he said, "We don't have too far to get to Hero. Just through the southeastern forest and past the towns of the Crossroads."

Anise knew that the Crossroads was the name of the loose confederation of towns and villages that included Hero. Still, it had never meant much to her. Almost all the village life of Hero was in Hero.

"Briac," she said. "I've been thinking. I'd like to stay here for a little while."

"Stay here?" said Briac, "are you serious?" He stared at her. "What's here to stay here for? And what about going home to Hero?"

"You probably don't remember," said Anise, "But I promised that I would help the people who needed help." She looked into his eyes. "The people these guards are catching and selling need my help."

She held one hand out, palm turned upward toward the sky. Iggy launched himself into the air. "I may not have the power to bring down lightning from the skies," she said, "but I can do this." Anise launched a burst of flame out of her palm, blasting upward toward the heavens. Iggy flew into the flaming updraft, twisting and turning like a salmon bounding up a mountain stream. The air grew chill around them.

"Burn," Iggy called out gleefully.

"At the least," said Anise, "I can make these Grisput guards regret what they are doing."

6

A nise started small. Her goal wasn't to kill all the guardsmen, who, even though they were part of the system, weren't solely responsible for maintaining or creating it. In so far as she had a goal, it was to give the leaders and slavers of Grisput the message that there was a cost to their actions.

She started ambushing small groups of Grisput guards when they were vulnerable. Briac watched and let her know when a suitable target was leaving the city. He was less recognizable than her and could blend in among the people entering and exiting.

They developed a system. Briac would wait by the main gate into Grisput, with Iggy as a wisp of smoke on his shoulder. When Briac saw a likely target for Anise, he would send Iggy off to alert her that the target was coming.

Iggy had at first been reluctant to do this. He hadn't wanted to give up his place near Anise. It seemed like he felt a need to stay close to her. But, Anise and Briac had convinced him that Briac's shoulder was also a welcome and comfortable place to stay.

They had convinced Iggy of this one evening by the campfire. Iggy was settled on Anise's shoulder when Briac started to play his lute. Iggy's body relaxed, his eyes closed, and he started his cat's purr. Anise carefully picked up his loose form and put him on Briac's shoulder, trying not to interfere with the lute playing. Iggy sighed and settled in a little deeper. He started kneading Briac's shoulder with his obsidian talons; Briac had winced and made an effort to keep playing.

Anise had some success with her small attacks. At

least the Guard seemed to be recognizing her presence. They stopped coming out in small groups. They started using the other entrances to come and go in a slightly worrisome development. Briac reported that the people he talked to on the roads and near the gate spoke about Death's Daughter quite a bit. Mostly favorably. Not surprisingly, the Grisput Guardsmen weren't too popular among the common folk.

One night around the campfire, Briac expressed some concerns.

"You know," he said, "They're not going to put up with this forever. Eventually, they're going to set a trap for you." He frowned. "I wouldn't be surprised if they try first with more troops, and then if that doesn't work, they'll probably hire some Academy mages to try to bring you down."

"Well," said Anise, "Maybe I should do something bigger before they get that chance."

7

Sebastian changed his mind about going straight to Ashton. Death's Daughter had to have something to do with Anise. The description he had overheard in Der Bunte Hund of the creature she had battled sounded just like one of the nightmares he had fought as the Knight of Moon & Shadow.

He searched the local area for word and news of Todes Tochter. He found himself traveling from town to town following news, hints, and rumors.

Hay-bale was very patient with the search. She carefully discussed what they should do with Sebastian in the evenings around their campfires. She would make her recommendations with grunts, whinnies, and neighs, but in the end, she let Sebastian decide what their course of action should be. Anise was his niece, after all.

Sebastian had plenty of time to think about the story he had heard back in Der Bunte Hund. The description of the creature that had attacked Death's Daughter had to be one of the nightmares that Lorenzo had used to attack the Knight of Moon & Shadow back in the day. Recognition of the creature and the method of attack brought him to a realization.

A building fury grew in Sebastian. It was Lorenzo. It had to be Lorenzo. It had always been Lorenzo. How had he ever thought that the jade heart he and Luna had used to transform the man had had a permanent effect? Something was wrong with him.

Sebastian wasn't sure how he knew that he had to talk to Death's Daughter about Anise; he just knew. He wondered if

Death's Daughter might be something like the Knight of Moon & Shadow, a channeled creation. Regardless, the connection with the nightmare had shown him what needed to be done next. The building rage he was feeling toward Lorenzo made him feel torn, but finding Anise took precedence over any revenge.

8

Briac was scouting for possible targets. He was under the shade of some trees away from the main gate out of the Grisput. The sun was starting to set, and the area right near the entrance was even darker as the cliffs below upper Grisput were casting their shadows on the city walls.

Briac was thinking about calling it a night. He was about to leave his watch-post to find where Anise had set up camp for the night when he saw a carriage and a group of armed men march out of the gate.

He waved his hand at the wisp of smoke on his shoulder.

"Iggy," he said urgently, "Go tell Anise that there's a group of men ...," he squinted at the troop, "Twenty or so, heading out of the main gate escorting a carriage. They're heading west. The carriage may have someone important in it."

The wisp of smoke firmed up into the shape of the fire imp. Iggy nodded eagerly at Briac, his face taking on a look of pride at the importance of his commission. He launched himself into the air, his wings flapping vigorously.

Anise was putting the finishing touches on her stack of firewood for the campfire when Iggy emerged from the sky. He alighted on her shoulder. The fire imp looked her in the face, pointed west with one obsidian claw, and said, "Burn." His wrinkled, leathery face acquired an expression of self-satisfaction for having fulfilled his assignment so well.

Because they had left the city late in the evening, the carriage and its escort of armed men hadn't gone far before setting up camp. Anise was just outside the circle of their campfires, watching them and wondering why they hadn't left the following day. They could have stayed in whatever cushy quarters they had in the city rather than camping in the woods.

While Anise was watching them, she heard a scurrying in the underbrush behind her. It was Briac. He was out of breath.

"Anise," he whispered urgently, "I'm glad I got here in time," He shook his head, "It's hard to see in the bad lighting, but they're not the Grisput Guard. I only noticed after I sent Iggy." He pointed to the tabards the guardsmen were wearing. Anise squinted to see one. They were not the purple with the black silhouette of the serpent that the Grisput guard wore, but rather the dark blue with the symbol of the wolf that represented the King's men.

9

Anise started to step forward into the circle of firelight. Briac put his hand on her arm to stop her, but she shook him off. She flipped her visor down over her face and moved out from the underbrush into the light.

The guardsmen stopped what they were doing and turned toward her. Most put their hands on their weapons. "Death's Daughter!" said one.

The carriage was off to one side of the guard's campground. There was a large tent, whose canvas walls were illuminated from the inside, in the center of the cleared area. Several fires were blazing around the clearing. A couple of the guardsmen stepped toward the tent entrance as Anise started to speak. Iggy faded into visibility on Anise's shoulder.

"I have no quarrel with the king's men," said Anise. With the visor down, her voice was again distorted and deepened. "But, I would like to know what you are doing coming out of Grisput, whose men I do have a quarrel with."

The guardsmen remained alert but didn't make any additional moves toward their weapons. One of the two who were near the tent slipped inside. Another man stepped forward.

"My lady," he said in a tone meant to be disarming, "as you can see, we owe our allegiance to the king and not to the rulers of Grisput." He gestured to the blue tabards with the wolf silhouette that they all wore. "We are escorting the king's Grisput envoy back to Capitol for a meeting with the king."

Briac stepped out of the shadows to stand behind Anise. One of the men started, but the somewhat delicate standoff held.

The man who had slipped into the tent reemerged. He bowed to Anise. "Your ladyship," he started. Anise wasn't sure where the title had come from, but perhaps they were just being careful. "Your ladyship. The king's envoy to Grisput requests an audience." He gestured to the open tent flap behind him.

Anise nodded and walked into the tent. Briac looked carefully from side to side at the armed men around them, then slowly followed her inside.

It was even dimmer inside than it had been outside. The light of a single oil lamp lit the interior of the tent. A camp bed with linen bedding was against one wall, and a portable desk was unfolded against the other. In between, a man was standing in the flickering light. He looked old to Anise, though she knew she would have to reassess her idea of what old was once she came to terms with having been asleep for fifteen years. He had red hair streaked with gray and startling green eyes that flashed with intelligence in the dim light.

"Death's Daughter," he said. "I've been hoping we'd get a chance to meet."

"Reynard?" said a flabbergasted Anise. Her voice echoed strangely through her helmet's visor.

10

The king's envoy to Grisput looked a little taken aback. "Yes, my name is Reynard," he said. "Do I know you?" He peered at Anise through the flickering lamplight. The death's head skull image on her helmet glimmered in the gloom.

Anise flipped up her visor. "Reynard, it is you." She smiled and stepped forward. "It's me, Anise. You remember, from Hero." Anise hadn't seen Reynard since before she had left Hero, which felt like an eternity ago. He'd been one of the first people she had met when she moved to town, as he and his friend William had been on guard duty when Aunt Rose brought her there.

"Hero?" said Reynard, "Oh, you mean Westhavenfieldbrook. That feels like such a long time ago." He shook his head. "Anise. Of course, I remember you. Didn't you have some kind of accident? I heard something about The Girl Who Dreamed."

"I got better," said Anise quietly.

Briac relaxed a little. The tension that had been in the air since Anise stepped into the clearing had eased. He glanced at the guardsmen standing at the sides of the tent flap just outside, and it seemed like they felt the lessening pressure as well.

"So tell me," said Reynard, smiling, "How is it that Anise from Westhavenfieldbrook is Death's Daughter?"

"Only if you tell me how Reynard from Hero came to be the King's Envoy to Grisput," said Anise with a matching grin.

Reynard got several folding chairs and a flask of wine from somewhere, and the three of them sat in his tent. Anise told her story. The relief of finding someone she could trust, someone from home, brought her comfort. She told her whole story in detail. Briac listened with interest as he hadn't heard some parts of what she had to tell. Iggy was less interested and expressed his disinterest with the occasional hiss or quiet seething growl.

When she had finished bringing Reynard up to date on what she was doing and what she was trying to do, he looked thoughtful.

"You know, Anise," he said, "Part of why I wanted to meet with you when I simply thought of you as Death's Daughter is still very relevant." He took a sip of wine from his cup. "I wanted to meet you and talk to you because we have business to discuss regarding your motives and methods in attacking Grisput." He pursed his lips and looked thoughtful. "I was going to try to dissuade you from your attacks on the Guard." He looked up and met her eyes. "Not because I think you're wrong. In fact, the king and I entirely share your motives. The indentured servitude system in Grisput is repugnant and needs to be stopped as soon as possible."

Reynard pressed his fingers together to form a steeple. "No, the problem is that your methods aren't working. The guard and the leaders of Grisput are just digging in their heels. They don't even really see it as connected to indentured servitude. They just see it as an attack on themselves. I thought I understood, so I wanted to talk to Death's Daughter before I knew she was you."

Reynard stood, stretched, and said, "So, if I may give you some fatherly advice." He smiled. "I think I know what you need to do. I think maybe you do as well." He sat back down again and leaned forward. "Twilight and I have the Grisput situation in hand, I hope. We're combining a campaign of education and information about how bad the system is with diplomatic pressure. I think we've been making some headway. I think you need to give up on attacking the Grisput Guard and go back to the Academy and confront Lorenzo. From your description of your adventures, I think it's clear that he is the one behind your troubles. I think he is the villain of your story. You know, I didn't trust him when Sebastian first told me about him years ago. I think it's been him all along."

11

Anise met Reynard's eyes. "So," she said, "Thank you for your advice. You've certainly given me something to think about." She smiled. "Now, I think it's your turn. What happened to you after the Knight of Moon & Shadow saved Westhavenfieldbrook? William kept talking about you for years."

"I feel bad about William," said Reynard. "I've been meaning to check on him." He frowned. "It's just I've been so busy."

"So, tell me," said Anise, "Last time I saw you, you were laid up in bed recovering from injuries the nightmare that attacked Hero had given you."

"Yes," said Reynard, "that took a lot of time. I had a lot of time to think." He laughed. "Too much time, I fear. I decided to see the world while I was still young. (And, I was still young. That was twenty years ago)."

He shook his head, "With the foolish imagined wisdom of youth, I decided to just leave. I didn't really talk to anyone. I thought people might try to talk me out of going." He looked up and met Anise's eyes. "There were quite a few times, later in life, when I labored under the bondage of Grisput when I wished they had."

"You were a bondsman?" said Anise. She noticed his left ear for the first time. A chunk of the earlobe was missing; it had healed long ago. She recognized the injury as the way a bondsperson from Grisput was marked.

Reynard put his hand to the clipped ear. "Yes," he said, "for years. There was a time when that's all I thought I would ever be." He wiggled the part of his ear where the earlobe should be with his fingers. "You know, this makes it harder to deal with the Grisput aristocracy. But, I kind of like that."

He laughed again. "Rub their noses in it, so to speak. Or, their ears."

Reynard continued, "Anyway, that's jumping ahead in the story. I left Hero with nothing but a backpack of supplies, a small amount of money, and high hopes."

Reynard stared into his wine cup. "I had some adventures. There were some good times and some bad. They ended, however, when I got to Grisput." He brightened. "At first, in a good way. I met a girl. That's why I didn't talk to William about leaving Hero, by the way. He'd already met Agnes. I didn't want to make him feel torn between her and me."

Reynard lifted his cup, took a sip, then continued, "The girl I met was everything I ever wanted. A copper-haired beauty. We were happy for what now seems like a very brief time. She lived in a little village not far from Grisput. We got married and started talking about a family. That's when the guard arrested me. They claimed for poaching. I heard she died a few years later."

He waved his hand in the air. "Enough about that. I was trapped in bondage for years. My king, my friend, Twilight, saved me from that fate. He saved me, and now we're doing everything we can to save everyone else who is held in this evil city."

12

Anise and Briac were sitting by their campfire. Iggy was lounging *in* the fire, relaxing and enjoying the heat. His presence made it harder to add a new piece of wood, but he moved every now and then, which stirred the flames, so they didn't have to use a stick as a poker to keep the fire blazing.

"I put something together while we were talking to Reynard," said Briac.

"What was that?" asked Anise. She was staring somewhat moodily into the fire, her thoughts lost in a morass. She had enjoyed the feeling of purpose that fighting with the Grisput guard had given her. So, while she thought Reynard was probably right, she didn't entirely like it.

"When you told him what Flambé, the dragon, said to you in your channeling dream. The part about the Keep and the Scrying Pool. You didn't tell me that part before."

Anise looked up from the flickering flames. "What about it?"

"The damaged journal of Drun Coeloc that I told you about? It mentioned both of those things. Both the Keep and the Scrying Pool."

"What did it say?" asked Anise.

"Not too much," said Briac, "But it seems significant now. It talked about a place called the Keep of Truth and Deceit. Apparently, it's on the Isle of the Wise."

"There's nothing on the Isle of the Wise but mist, gravel paths, and mystery," said Anise.

Briac shook his head. "Not according to master Coeloc," he said. "And the Scrying Pool? He mentions that too. In fact, though he doesn't say what it is, he makes it sound pretty important. Apparently, the opening of the Scrying Pool is what made him go to the academy. It wasn't clear why, but that was a tipping point."

Anise was silent. They both gazed into the fire. Then, it was Briac's turn to look up and catch her attention. "Another thing," he continued. Anise groaned audibly. "You know it's time. You've been putting it off for too long. I know it's hard, sometimes, to talk to family, but they've got to be worried sick. You need to reach out."

13

Something woke Sebastian, and he sat up. He glanced at the smoldering embers of his campfire. He had banked it so it wouldn't spread, but he hadn't doused it completely, as the warmth was still welcome while he slept.

He looked for Hay-bale but didn't see her. Then he noticed some other strange things. The stars weren't the same constellations he was familiar with. And the glow of glimmering light from the coals seemed to form a perfect circle around his campsite.

He recognized this. This was how his dreams had looked when he'd been the Knight of Moon & Shadow. When he'd met with Luna on his quest.

Sebastian rose to his feet and looked around. A figure moved at the edge of the campsite and stepped into the light. A woman's shape, dressed in black, with a skull for a face.

"Death's Daughter," breathed Sebastian. He put his hand on his sword-hilt.

The woman moved closer. She grasped the bottom of the skull visage and lifted it, revealing Anise's face underneath. "Uncle Sebastian," she said. She ran towards him, collapsing into his arms in a deathly tight embrace and bursting into tears.

"Anise?" said Sebastian, holding the sobbing woman in his arms.

"I'm so sorry," said Anise. "I've been meaning to tell you, Rose, and Isabel that I'm all right. There's just been so much going on, and it's been so long."

Sebastian wiped a tear off Anise's face. "It's all right," he said, "I'm just glad you're safe." He looked around. "Are you safe?" he asked. "And, where are we?"

"We're in your dream," said Anise. "I'm a dream walker,"

she continued proudly.

"Anise," said Sebastian, "Where are you in the waking world? I've been looking for you."

"Don't worry about me," said Anise. "I've figured out what I need to do to end this. I'm going to the Academy, to a place called The Keep of Truth and Deceit. I'm going to confront Master Lorenzo." She shook her head. "He's the one who trapped me in the dream realm."

"When I heard about that nightmare beast that attacked you, I thought it must be him," said Sebastian. "I can't believe I trusted him. I was so sure he had reformed."

Anise looked worried. "Don't try to follow me to the keep," she said. "I need to finish this myself." She touched her uncle's hand. "I'll come home to you, Rose, and Isabel, in Hero when this is all over."

ASHTON

1

The third dream storm struck during the first hours of darkness. Anise and Briac were asleep at their campsite. Iggy stirred restlessly even before the first crack presaged the crackling sound. Sebastian shifted in his sleep at his own campsite to the north but managed to sleep through the noises.

Anise sat bolt upright when the crack happened. The sound felt like it was cutting into her brain. She put both hands to the sides of her head and pressed. Briac woke a bit less quickly. He looked around the campsite groggily.

There was a loud rustling in the underbrush near them. Anise stood and lit the area with a cool conjured sphere of master Videmon's light.

A creature burst through the trees into the clear, knocking one of the smaller trees to the ground as it did so. Briac leapt to his feet, looking to the ground near the bedroll for his dagger.

It was a nightmare. Like the one Anise had fought back on the road near the Dragon River. Somehow Anise felt like the creature didn't understand why it was here. As if it was lost and confused. It didn't matter, however. It raised its forelimbs and charged toward the embers of their campfire and them.

Iggy launched himself into the air. He maintained a respectful distance as he remembered what had happened the last time he had tangled with one of these creatures. He blasted his fiery breath at the beast. The flames washed over it like water without effect.

Anise faced the creature. The crackling sound filled the clearing. She knew that it was a creature out of a dream. She had a sudden inspiration. Starting with the image of the circle of light that channelers manipulated in their dreams, she formed the glowing sphere she had conjured into a band of illumination. Gesturing with both hands, she moved the hoop of light between her and Briac and the creature. She tried to imbue the gleaming ring with the same connection to the dreaming world that permeated the circle of light in a channeling dream.

Iggy started flapping his wings furiously to backpedal away from the circle. He looked scared. The creature stopped its forward charge and just stared at the glowing band.

Anise thrust her hands forward toward the creature, moving the ring of illumination at and over it. The beast vanished as the light surrounded it, back into the dream it had come from.

Sebastian woke with tears in his eyes and sweat dampening his armpits. He sat up and rubbed his face with his hands. There was some strange crackling sound, faintly sounding in the distance, but it faded as he listened. As the crackling sound faded, Sebastian heard the distant cry of a wolf. He knew why he had been weeping. For the first time in years, he'd had the dream again. He'd dreamt of the day he, Isabel, and their infant son had gone on an outing to the forest. The weather had been so lovely and the day so warm that he and Isabel had fallen asleep on their spread blanket near their food basket.

The dream hadn't ended there, though the next part was less memory and more nightmare. Sebastian dreamt he was somehow following his infant son as he toddled off into the woods away from his parents.

His dream had forced him to watch as his little Twilight bumbled into a clearing filled with wolves. The nightmare had ended with the slavering wolves charging at his little boy.

2

Sebastian was riding Hay-bale through the streets of Lakeside. A small town across the lake from Ashton and the Academy, Lakeside had never been very interesting to Sebastian. It was just a town you rode through on your way to the other side of the lake.

This time what struck him about the town was how many clairvoyance students from the Academy had set up shop here. The symbol for a clairvoyant trying to sell their services was a wooden or iron sign of an eye hanging above the doorway. It felt to Sebastian like every second house in town had one.

The shops were shuttered, though it was almost midday. Also, as it had been in Brierstock, the streets were more empty than usual. Though he suspected he might already know the answer, Sebastian asked a passing woman why all the clairvoyants' shops were closed.

"The dreams affected them more than everyone else," the woman answered.

Sebastian nodded. Though it hadn't felt dangerous, not to him at least, the dream that had woken him the night before had been more real and immediate than any dream he had ever had before.

The ride from Lakeside to Ashton was pleasant. The sun shone on the trail and reflected off the lake's waters. Hay-bale was in a good mood and listened attentively to Sebastian's musings.

"Should I confront Lorenzo or try to find the Keep of Truth and Deceit?" said Sebastian.

Hay-bale nickered.

Sebastian looked thoughtful, "You're right," he said. "Anise might be annoyed if I try to confront Lorenzo without her here." He nodded. "I'll try to find out something about the Keep."

3

Sebastian and Hay-bale rode into Ashton just as the sun started to set. The Dragon Watchtower stood out against the skyline. There was still some scaffolding on one side of the rebuilt tower, but it looked almost complete. The last time Sebastian had been here, visiting his sleeping niece, the tower's reconstruction had just started. Sebastian thought he saw a ballista standing atop the distant tower.

More people were wandering the streets of Ashton than there had been in Lakeside. The citizens of this town were more used to unusual happenings, being closer to the Academy. Maybe, whatever had happened the day before hadn't had as much effect on them.

Sebastian saw a group of men in the uniforms of the Dragon Watch. The red tabard over a leather jerkin, with the silhouette of a dragon's head on the chest, was familiar. But, these men were acting quite differently than the friendly night watchman he remembered from his first visit here. There were five of them walking close together. At least one of them always kept an eye on the sky, and they all were alert.

Sebastian walked down Dead Man's Alley past the open windows of the Greedy Gull inn. They had just lit the lamps to brighten the darkening twilight. The Inn's common room, glimpsed through the open windows, looked warm and inviting, and Sebastian was tempted to stop in and say hello to Swen, the innkeeper, and his daughter. But that wasn't his destination. He clucked to Hay-bale and pulled gently on the reins to distract her from the warmth and the light.

They turned off a cross street onto Leafdrop Lane a little further on. Sebastian let Hay-bale pick her own pace. He always felt welcomed, but he didn't like asking for favors, so he wasn't in any hurry.

A row of unassuming houses came into view. The one with faded green paint and a battered old oak door with the number thirteen carved into it didn't stand out from the rest. Sebastian pulled Hay-bale to a stop, dismounted, and approached the door.

Holding Hay-bale's reins in one hand, he reached out the other and rapped on the oak wood of the door.

4

The door opened. Sebastian had to adjust his gaze down to the top of a head of bright red hair and a pair of emerald eyes gazing up at him. Hay-bale nickered, hopefully. Unlike Betsy, who had mistrusted new people on sight, Hay-bale assumed they would give her something to eat.

"Sebastian," called out Maeve breathlessly. She hugged him around the thighs.

Sebastian put out the hand that wasn't holding Hay-bale's reins and grabbed the door frame for balance. "Hello, Maeve," he responded a little less emphatically but warmly.

"You're here because of Anise," said Maeve.

"Of course," said Sebastian.

Almost simultaneously, they both continued, "Have you heard anything?"

Sebastian nodded. "I haven't seen her, but she contacted me in a dream." He looked thoughtful. "So I guess I did see her. Though I'm not sure if that counts or not. Anyway, she said she was coming here to go to someplace called the Keep of Truth and Deceit."

"The Keep of Truth and Deceit?" said Maeve. "That's all anyone talks about anymore. Master Lorenzo has been making a big deal about it like he discovered it. He could have asked me about it, and I would have told him where it was."

A young man dressed in a disheveled cook's uniform burst into the otherwise empty common room. He was young to Sebastian's eyes, though he must have been in his mid to late twenties. He was thin but looked strong. He charged over to the doorway where Sebastian and Maeve were and said, "Where is she? Is she with you?" His red hair flopped over his eyes, making him look a little crazed.

Maeve frowned. She turned to Sebastian apologetically and said, "You remember Raphael, our cook?"

5

Sebastian looked inquisitively at the young man. "She's not with me," he said. "I haven't seen her yet, but I heard that she's on her way here." He nodded at the young man in his kitchen rumpled uniform. "Didn't you used to be a skinny little kid?"

The young man grunted noncommittally and turned and left the way he came, through the door that led toward the way-house kitchens.

"You'll have to forgive Raphael," said Maeve. "He's been a bit distraught since Anise woke up." She looked thoughtful. "He was quite conscientious about visiting her while she was asleep. I think he made the trip to the infirmary at least once a week."

Maeve met Sebastian's eyes. "Anyway," she said, "Why would Anise be thinking about going to the Keep of Truth and Deceit?"

"I don't know, exactly," said Sebastian. "She said she was going to go there to confront Lorenzo."

"What does she want to confront Lorenzo about?" asked Maeve.

Sebastian looked angry. "It was him, Maeve. He was the one who trapped Anise in the dream world. He's the one who made her lose fifteen years of her life."

Maeve looked shocked. "But, why?" she said.

"There's something wrong about how he's thinking," said Sebastian. "He's obsessed with a prophecy that he heard years ago. He thinks Anise is some kind of dark channeler who will doom the world."

"Well," said Maeve, "that doesn't sound right." She

frowned. "Maybe I'll have to talk to some of my connections at the Academy."

"I don't think we should do anything until Anise gets here," said Sebastian. "I was just going to try to find out something about this 'Keep of Truth and Deceit' for her."

"Well," said Maeve, "the Keep of Truth and Deceit is where Lorenzo spends most of his time nowadays." She made a tut-tutting noise. "Ever since he 'discovered' the Keep, it's all they talk about at the Academy. 'We've found the heart of the dreaming.' 'Clairvoyants now know where their paths begin.'"

"You sound skeptical," said Sebastian.

"Well," said Maeve, "as I said, if he'd asked me, I could have told him that there was a castle on the Isle of the Wise long ago." She shook her head. "But no one thought to ask me."

"If I might ask," said Sebastian, "Where does your knowledge come from?"

"And well, you might," said Maeve. Her voice took on a formal tone that Sebastian hadn't heard before, her gaze grew a little distracted, and she began to recite.

6

I t felt a little like Maeve was talking to someone more than Sebastian. Like she was speaking to her people or her family as well, though there was no one else in the room. "This is a tale my people have told since the time before you móra overshadowed these lands. From when our folk filled the land from the sea to the Etenies mountains. It is sometimes called 'the Queen who ruled from Dream.'

"The weak spot between the worlds, the place where dream meets existence, is a fort. It is built of a stone, not from the earth, crafted by someone there before anyone was there. The keep is where dream creatures meet those from our world who wander too far away from wakefulness."

Maeve looked up to meet Sebastian's eyes. "My people have known to shun the keep and the island for ages. We didn't always know this.

"There was a queen in those days, Coblaith. She was the ruler of the clan that lived in this region. Most of the women of my people are wiser than the men, but she was an ambitious prideful woman. She almost resembled a man in some ways." Maeve winked at Sebastian.

"The fort is on the island, and there is no way to get there except by boat. There is no bridge, no causeway, no way to walk. Swimmers don't seem to make it, though it's unknown exactly why.

"At a time when the keep was empty, abandoned, Coblaith took her people, her clan, on boats to the island. They moved into the keep and set up house there.

"For several years, Coblaith's kin prospered and grew strong and populous. They expanded their reach and power, conquering neighboring clans. Corblaith must have achieved some of her ambitions.

"They also grew strange. The people of the neighboring clans had to work with them and deal with them due to their power and influence, but tales sung to this day tell of how distant and eerily they behaved. As if living on the island and in the keep had changed them somehow.

"The story doesn't end well, as you might imagine," continued Maeve. "One day, the people of Coblaith's clan just disappeared. Scouts from the neighboring clans were sent to check on the island and the keep. They found the fort empty, looking exactly as before it was occupied."

Maeve sighed. "That was enough for my people. We have long memories. None of my folk have been to the Isle of the Wise for hundreds of years."

7

Maeve looked around the empty common room. "Cian," she called out. "Come greet Anise's uncle!" She turned to Sebastian. "Cian still lives here," she said. "Mostly to keep her old mother company, I think." She winked at Sebastian. "She's done well for herself with her Academy education. She's a house-keeper."

"A house-keeper," said Sebastian, impressed. "We haven't had a house-keeper in Hero in years. I think the Mayor had one a few years back for a little while. But that was mostly for show, and I don't think he had ever been anywhere near the Academy."

Cian stepped into the room from the back hall. She was a larger version of her mother, with the same emerald eyes and flaming red hair.

"Uncle Sebastian," she said. She came over and gave him a hug. "Have you heard anything about Anise?"

"I know that she's alive, and she's on her way here," said Sebastian. Cian looked relieved. "Your mother tells me you're a house-keeper now?"

"She's not just a house-keeper," said Maeve. "She's been hired by some of the wealthiest people in town." Maeve was practically glowing with pride. "She's had to hire helpers. One of the masters from the Academy has been talking about hiring her to keep his house."

"Mother!" said Cian. The exasperation was evident in her voice.

"So, what services do you offer?" asked Sebastian.

It was Cian's turn to look proud. "We're a full-service keeping business," she said. "Security, lighting, maintenance, construction. We can cast a good luck charm to ensure the fortune of all the house's residents or a vigor one to maintain good health. Our motto is 'If you want to keep your house, hire us as house-keepers.'" She frowned. "I know it's not very good yet. It's still a work in progress."

After assuring Cian that he would pass on the information if any news about Anise came up, Sebastian turned back to Maeve.

"So, how do I get into the Keep of Truth and Deceit?"

8

Maeve looked thoughtful. "Our people do have other stories about the keep," she said. "more myth than history. It is said that the keep used to be the stronghold of the lord of dreams. I believe you móra call him Morpheus. He built it, of course, before the time of Coblaith. Before the time of my people in general, and certainly before yours. He abandoned it, moving on to somewhere else later. His former presence there made the Isle of the Wise a thin spot between our world and Dream."

"That doesn't help me get in," said Sebastian sadly.

"I'm not done yet." Maeve sighed with exasperation. "The main gates are called the Gates of Horn and Ivory. They stand side by side, but the story is that they can only be opened by a mage, a wizard, by magic."

"But, your story about Coblaith and her people?" asked Sebastian.

"Just because my people are different doesn't mean we don't have magic," said Maeve. "It works a bit differently than your Academy trained mages, but it works well."

Sebastian shook his head. "Still doesn't help me." He waved his hands up and down a little mournfully. "Whatever magic I had, if it was ever mine, left me a long time ago when I put the moon back up into the sky."

Maeve shot Sebastian a look. Cian looked away so as not to come anywhere near meeting Maeve's eyes, but Sebastian was oblivious.

"If I may continue," she said and waited a moment. Sebastian didn't say anything. "There is another entrance."

Sebastian looked attentive and quiet, and Maeve continued, "let me tell you a tale of Galan, known, among other names, as Galan dream-stealer."

9

Maeve started into her tale. Cian's eyes snapped to her mother's face. She focused on her mother's expression and her words. Something *was* captivating about the sound of Maeve's voice, thought Sebastian, as he lost himself in the story as well.

"Now Galan Dream-stealer was a great hero of our people, but this was in the days before that. He was just a young boy on the verge of manhood, living in a village where Lakeside is now. The people of his settlement already knew to avoid the island. Though, this was before the time of Corblaith and her occupation of the keep.

"They avoided the island and the keep because they knew that the lord of dreams lived there."

"I thought you said he abandoned it?" asked Sebastian. Cian's jaw dropped open a bit, and she stared at him.

Maeve looked a little disgruntled. "This was before that," she said. "The lord of dreams still lived there when Galan was young. Perhaps this story has something to do with why he left."

She looked up at Sebastian. He found the expression in her emerald green eyes hard to read. From the way Cian reacted, it seemed she understood it better. "If I may?" she said. Sebastian nodded.

"Now, there was a girl in the village. It's not clear if she was anything special. History and the stories don't tell us much about her. But, to Galan, she was. He thought the sun shone down onto the earth just for her. They were due to get married. Galan was ready to make her his wife and give her the happy village life she wanted.

"But as young people sometimes do, she had doubts. She expressed them to him by describing her dreams. She told

Galan that she was dreaming of another young man in the village. This other young man was a successful hunter and quite a charmer, and many of the girls in the village dreamed about him in many different ways. Galan didn't consider whether the dreaming she was talking about might be less than literal. He just took her at her word. He blamed the dream for the problem, not the girl."

10

Maeve continued, "Now, being the young man destined to turn into the hero he was to become, Galan didn't react to this the way another man might. He blamed the dream, but he knew where it came from and who had sent it.

"He took one of the small fishing boats that his people used to fish the lake's waters and set out toward the island you now call the Isle of the Wise."

Maeve shook her head. "The people of Galan's village knew better than to approach the island of the lord of dreams. Still, Galan was destined to become a hero, and the difference between a hero and a fool can sometimes be as narrow as a sharp knife's blade.

"The mists were heavy around the island. Perhaps even more than they are now. It's said that the curtain between the realm of Dream and the world was thinner while the dream lord lived in his keep. The mists were heavy, but Galan was resolute. He drew his boat onto the island's shore after a timeless age drifting in the fog on the lake waters.

"He knew what he was looking for. His people told tales of the lord of dream's keep, but the mists were thicker on the shores. There are separate stories told of his time in the mists trying to find the keep," Maeve looked up at Sebastian and met his eyes. "But, I know that you are impatient to get the answer to your question, so I'll leave those stories for another time," she continued.

"Just let it be known that Galan Dream-Stealer, hero of song and story, made it through the mists and stood before the Gates of Horn and Ivory.

"Now, like you, Galan was no channeler, no mage. He was just a boy looking to bring a girl back into his dreams. He had no way to open either gate.

"He tried the gates, both of them. He shook them, rattled them, and called out until he was hoarse, but the gates wouldn't budge, and there was no one there in the mist but him.

"Once he realized he wasn't getting in that way, Galan started looking for another entrance. To the main gates' right, low on the wall behind some bushes, he found his access, his way in.

"My people call it the Gate of Heros, but it's just a sewer system, a crawlway. Though what or who that lives in the lord of dreams' keep needs a sewer, I don't know."

11

Sebastian made a move as if to turn away. "Thank you, Ma ...," he started to say. Cian made a motion with her finger to her lips. She didn't have to make the shushing noise. It was implicit in the gesture.

"You're not thinking about leaving before the story is done," she whispered urgently. Her statement was structured like a question but sounded more like a command. Maeve seemed oblivious. She continued.

"Galan made his way into the keep through the gate of heroes. Once inside the keep, he had to decide where to go. The stories our people told at that time spoke of the Dream-lord keeping watch over the realms of reality and dream from a high room in the keep. So, Galan decided to make his way up toward the top of the fort.

"The keep was like a maze of convoluted corridors and passageways, and Galan's path was complicated by needing to avoid the Dream-lord's servants. Some didn't look too different from the villagers in Galan's village. Others were little winged folk who flapped their tiny bat-like wings as they flitted through the stone corridors about their lord's business.

"Every time Galan came across a stair, he climbed it. Every time he encountered a servant of the dream lord, he hid. Eventually, he reached a large room toward the top of the keep with a wide-open double door. At the entrance to the door was a tall thin man wearing a flowing black robe. He turned his pale face to Galan before he had time to hide and said, 'Ah, Galan, I've been waiting for you. Come with me. I've got something to show you.'

"The need for hiding clearly gone, Galan followed the pale lord of dreams into the room behind him. It was a large room, though the full extent was unclear. The far reaches stretched off to what must be the edges of the keep. The ceiling was open to the sky, though that sky was just a swirling expanse of mist. Both the walls and the floor were covered with doors and portals of every shape and size.

"The dream lord brought Galan over to a stone pool on the floor. He swept one arm over the murky greenish fluid in the basin. 'My scrying pool,' he said proudly. 'I've just built it. Look in. There is something that I think you should see.'

"Galan gazed into the murky fluid. At first, there was nothing but darkness, then his vision cleared, and he felt that he was looking into a clearing in the forest. He recognized the place; it wasn't far from his village. There, lit by the moon's light, was his girl in the arms of his rival, the young hunter. Galan realized that the girl of his dreams wasn't dreaming of him as he was dreaming of her.

"It's said," continued Maeve, "that that moment is what released Galan from a common fate as a villager. That moment inspired him to leave his village and go out and become the hero he was to become."

12

Briac, Anise, and Iggy were leaving Brierstock. Anise had gotten a long hooded cloak and wore it when they passed through towns. Her armor and appearance were distinctive enough that she felt it was better to conceal them to remain unrecognized. Iggy did his part by fading into a wisp of smoke on her shoulder. When they walked through the marketplace in Brierstock, Briac greeted everyone and chatted with all the shopkeepers.

As they left the city behind them and set out on the dusty road, Anise turned to her smiling companion. "You know, it doesn't help me keep undercover to have you talking to everyone," she said.

"Sorry," said Briac, though his smile said otherwise. "we haven't discussed what will happen when we get to Ashton," he continued.

Anise frowned. "I'm not exactly sure," she said. "I need to confront Lorenzo." Her brow furrowed. "He's evidently willing to resort to violence to get his way. I hope it doesn't have to come to that."

"Should we just walk into the Academy and ask to meet with him?" said Briac.

Anise shook her head. "I have no idea who's working with him or who to trust. I think we should get in the way I got out. We'll sneak in by the cover of darkness, borrow a boat from the docks, and row over to the Isle of the Wise. If we can find this Keep, and especially the Scrying Pool, we might be able to stop Lorenzo from whatever he's doing."

"Sounds like a plan," said Briac. "My orders are to get you to your final destination, and help you when you get there, so I'm just following you."

Anise's expression lightened. "Thank you, Briac. I don't

really know what I'm doing or why. But, you being with me has made doing it a lot easier."

Briac lifted her hand to his lips and kissed it. "That's what I'm here for," he said. Iggy looked skeptical.

13

Anise, Iggy, and Briac crossed the Scute bridge over the Dragon River. Behind them was the road that led north toward Meara and the ocean and south toward Brierstock. The way forward led toward Ashton, the Academy, and the Isle of the Wise.

Someone was walking toward them from the other side of the bridge. Anise pulled her cloak's hood forward over her head to hide her hair and the death's head helmet. She and Briac had become a little more casual on the road, especially when passing people traveling alone. But, she still felt the need to not draw attention to herself. Iggy hissed a little and faded from view on Anise's shoulder.

The person approaching them looked a little unusual. He was a tall young man, muscular and fit. He wore a cook's uniform and had a hefty cleaver stuck through his belt. There was an obviously improvised leather sheath around the cleaver blade. The razor-sharp edge was already cutting through the leather. He had some kind of hat perched on his head made out of metal.

As he walked closer, Anise inspected his face. He was handsome. Strands of red hair poked out from under the metal hat. He was tall, and her eyes were drawn to how his shoulders and biceps filled out the beige cook's uniform.

"Raffy?" said Anise.

The young man frowned. "No one calls me that," he said, "except ...," his eyes widened.

Anise pulled back her hood, stepped forward, and hugged Raphael. She felt the strength in his body under his cook's uniform as she squeezed him.

"Anise," said Raphael. "I was looking for you."

It was Briac's turn to frown. "So," he said, "Who is this?"

Anise stepped back a step. "Briac," she said, "You remember Raphael. From the Way-house? Raffy, I can't believe how big you've gotten."

"Of course," said Briac. "The cook's assistant. Didn't you used to be a skinny little kid?"

"I'm the cook now," said Raphael proudly.

"Is that a pot on your head?" asked Briac.

14

Raphael flushed. For a moment, his cheek's redness matched the color of the hair wisps that poked out from under the metal. "I lined it with cloth and banged it into shape with a hammer," he said. "I didn't have a helmet."

"Why did you need a helmet?" said Briac. Then he laughed. "Oh, I see. You're a knight coming to rescue your lady fair. How noble."

Anise glared at the bard. "Briac, be nice," she said. "Raffy, I'm so glad to see you," she said to Raphael. "I think your helmet looks very good."

Iggy faded into view on Anise's shoulder. Raphael jerked back and made a motion to reach for his cleaver. Anise reached out her hand and put it on Raphael's. "It's all right, Raffy," she said, "This is Iggy." She smiled at the worry on Raphael's face. "Iggy, say hi to Raphael." The fire imp hissed and focused his cat-like eyes on Raphael. "Burn," he said emphatically.

* * *

"So, out for a stroll, are you?" said Briac. Anise shot him a look.

"I was coming out to look for Anise," said Raphael, "to help. When she left Ashton, I knew she had to be scared of something. Maybe the same thing that made her sleep for so long."

"Well, you were right, Raffy," said Anise firmly. "It was master Lorenzo. I'm going back to Ashton to confront him."

"Master Lorenzo?" asked Raphael. He looked thoughtful. "There *was* something strange about how he stared at you when he came to the infirmary." Raphael gazed at Anise. "I'm coming with you," he said. He spoke quietly and calmly, but the way he said it felt like it left little room for argument. Briac frowned.

Anise looked worried. "Raffy," she said, "it could be dangerous. Lorenzo isn't who he's been pretending to be at the Academy. He's a dangerous man who is quite willing to use violence to get his way." She looked sad. "He killed my parents and left me lost in a dream. Uncle Sebastian thought he had put him right, but it didn't take."

Raphael met Anise's eyes and repeated, "I'm coming with you."

THE ISLE OF THE WISE

1

Sebastian didn't tell the fisherman renting him the boat everything. He felt bad about this, as he didn't like lying. Still, he wasn't strictly lying but simply omitting small parts of the truth. Not everyone needed to know everything.

The fisherman scowled at him. "Don't go into the mists," he said, gesturing out over the waters toward the fog-shrouded island in the distance. "Every now and then, some idiot rows too close to that island. It takes them a long time to come back, and sometimes they don't." He coughed and spat off the rustic wooden dock into the water.

Sebastian had left Hay-bale stabled in the Way-house's stable facilities. Sometimes some of the residents had horses. Maeve hired space for them in a livery barn just down the street from the Way-house. Cian promised to check in on Hay-bale and ensure she was all right. Sebastian rubbed her nose and told her he would be back soon. He wasn't sure she believed him, but she nickered her acknowledgment of his promise.

The boat Sebastian was hiring was a rough-looking rowboat. The fisherman looked even a little rougher than the boat, but the price was right, or, at least, what Sebastian could afford. He hadn't brought much money. Truth be told, he didn't have much. Being the Hero of Hero wasn't a paying gig, and small-town farmers didn't usually deal much in currency.

"You've been in a boat before?" said the man. Sebastian caught himself staring at the man's beard. The hair color had a hint of blue in it. It was a very unusual color. The fisherman noticed his gaze. "I moved here from Meara," he said without further word of explanation.

"Of course," said Sebastian. "My father used to take me fishing." His first lie of omission. His father had taken him fishing a few times, but they'd cast from the banks of the Westhaven river and hadn't caught much. The second lie of omission was inherent in the first. The only time he'd ever been on a boat was one time when he, Gerard, Leonard, and Isabel had stolen a rowboat when they were children. It had been Gerard's idea. It hadn't worked out too well, as they had spent the whole time trying to recapture one of the oars that fell off the side, got caught in the current, and drifted off downstream.

Sebastian got into the boat, trying to look smooth handling the oars as he put them into the oarlocks. The fisherman watched him skeptically. "Don't do anything too stupid," he said as he put his foot against the side of the rowboat and pushed it off from the dock.

Sebastian could practically hear the gears turning in the fisherman's head as he weighed the value of the money he had been paid against the possibility of losing his boat.

2

Sebastian rowed the small boat into the lake. He wasn't sure why people made such a big deal out of seamanship; this rowing stuff was easy. It had taken him a bit to get the pattern of pulling harder on one side when you wanted to turn. He had felt the eyes of the fisherman burning into him while he was still close to the dock, but now he had it.

The misty shores of the island felt like they were a long way off, but there was nothing for it except to put his back into it. Sebastian was used to hard work on his farm. Still, the rowing was unfamiliar, and after a short while, he felt like he was using other muscles than he was used to. Also, even though he had a farmer's calloused hands, the oars were hitting different parts of his palms.

At first, it was a relief when the rowboat entered the mists around the island. He had worked up a bit of a sweat in the morning sunshine, and the cool fog felt refreshing on his warm back. He glimpsed trees above the low-lying fog as the boat entered it, so he thought the island's shore couldn't be far. He continued rowing straight through the dense mist, trying to veer as little as possible.

Sebastian kept waiting for the boat to run aground or for there to be something to see other than pearly fog. He turned his head to see what was in front of the rowboat. He had known enough about rowing to sit with his back toward the boat's bow, so he had to crane his neck around to glimpse the front. There was nothing but the milky-white mist.

The sun went from a yellow spot in the fog overhead to a distant glow. The cool mist started feeling less friendly and more ominous. The only sound was the splashing of Sebastian's oars.

It got murky and chill. The dried sweat dampening the

back of Sebastian's tunic felt clammy and cold. He shivered. There was no sign of anything but the impenetrable fog. A strong smell came with the mist, like the smell of freshly unearthed moss from near the roots of an oak tree.

Sebastian firmed his grip on the oars, ignoring his new blisters, and put his back into rowing the boat forward.

3

Anise was crouched by the outside of the Academy wall. She was reaching out with her mind to try to contact the elemental strength of the volcano that was the Key to the elements. It wasn't hard. As soon as she reached for it, she felt the flowing lava, the turbulent moat around the mountain, and the surging winds above the caldera.

"I still don't understand why we didn't just walk in through the gates," said Raphael.

"I want to make sure there's no chance that Lorenzo knows we're coming," said Anise distractedly, "He has his ways, and I'd like to not give him time to prepare." She started to route the power of the magma in the volcano into the rock in front of her. A round hole began to form in the flowing stone. Iggy faded into view, launched himself off her shoulder, and did a joyful barrel roll in the air over her head.

Raphael gasped as the smooth stone of the wall flowed and shifted. Briac looked on in fascination. "I've been learning to do some magic with my music," he said. "But, nothing like that."

Anise grunted. Manipulation of elements, especially earth, was a bit draining. "I meant to ask you about that," she said as she rose to her feet. "What sort of things can you do?"

"Another time," said Briac. He glanced at Raphael a little skeptically.

After peering through to make sure that the coast was clear on the other side, Anise squeezed her way through the hole she had made. Briac and Raphael followed. They were screened from the rest of the Academy campus by a small grove of trees. Anise had seen the treetops above the wall.

"I've been meaning to tell you how nice it is to see you,

Raffy," said Anise. "I haven't been able to see anyone from the old days since I woke up."

Briac muttered, "Uh ...," and slightly lifted his hand.

"I'm surprised you didn't see Jord," said Raphael. "She was there almost every time I came to visit."

"Jord?" said Anise. "Why was Jord there?"

"Oh, you didn't hear?" said Raphael. "Jord's a master at the Academy now. In fact, she's the headmaster of the new Healing discipline."

4

The boats on the mist-shrouded dock were all locked up. The locks and chains were solid iron, thick and strong. Anise studied them. There was a reason why iron had a reputation as being resistant to magic. It was a tricky material to work with elemental skills. And, it tended to dispel illusions when they touched it. That was probably the reason why it was used on these locks. It would be challenging for the students to "borrow" these boats.

"I can work my way through these chains," said Anise, lowering her voice, "But it will take a while." She shook her head. "Shaping iron is really hard."

The three of them had made their way to the docks on the lake carefully and stealthily. Anise considered trying to hide their appearance with illusions. But, the Academy was the place in Liamec where there was most likely to be someone capable of "disbelieving" illusions. So, it was perhaps the place where they would be least effective.

"Wait a minute," said Briac, "let me." He pulled his backpack off his back and pulled out his lute.

"I'm not sure if this is the right time for a song," whispered Anise urgently.

Briac smiled. "It's always the right time for a song."

Raphael kept glancing over his shoulder in the direction of the fog obscured building at the end of the wharf. He seemed to feel guilty about sneaking around the campus. He looked especially worried about Anise trying to "liberate" one of the boats.

Briac strummed his lute quietly and began singing in a low voice. The song's words were in some language Anise had never heard before, but she felt something, some stirring of power. It reminded her of when Briac had come to the

Academy and conjured illusions with a song. Iggy sagged against Anise's shoulder and started making a noise like a cat's purr.

There was a gentle click as the padlock on the iron chain opened. Anise had the feeling the lock had been moved by Briac's voice.

"How did you do that?" she whispered. "I felt something, but it wasn't like any of the magic disciplines they teach at the academy."

"Music unlocks both hearts and locks," said Briac.

5

The oarlocks creaked as if they were complaining about the work Sebastian was putting them through. The blisters on his hands got so sore that he took out his pocket-handkerchief, ripped it in half, and bound half around each palm to be able to keep rowing.

Sebastian was confident that he was going straight, but it felt like he'd been rowing for hours, and there was no change in the pearly white fog that shrouded the lake's surface and the boat's gunwales. At this point, he would have welcomed the sound of the rowboat crashing into a rock. Anything to indicate that there was an end to the misty open waters.

Sebastian had plenty of time to think while he pulled on the oars. One thought that kept coming back was, "Why am I here?" Of course, the obvious answer was to help Anise, but he wasn't entirely sure he would be much use.

When he'd confronted Lorenzo before, as the Knight of Moon & Shadow, he'd had lots of help. He'd had Luna and Moonbeam guiding him. He'd had the gifts of his fellow villagers from Westhavenfieldbrook. He'd had his youth. Sebastian sighed. He wasn't that old now, but he certainly didn't have the confidence that inexperience gave the very young.

He pulled again firmly on the oars, ignoring the flare of pain he felt in his palms. It didn't matter. He would do what he could to help, even if it wasn't very much. Perhaps he could distract the enemy. Maybe he could throw himself in front of a fiery blast from Lorenzo's fingers, launched at Anise. Whatever he could do to help, he would.

There was a crunching sound as the boat's prow ran up onto a beach of water-smoothed pebbles. The rowboat came to an abrupt halt, and Sebastian was thrown backward. His palms ached again as he caught himself against the side.

He worried about the fisherman's boat. Sebastian climbed out and pulled it up onto the shore, inspecting the prow as he did. It didn't look like the hull had been damaged by the impact.

He looked around. The milky fog was still thick, and he couldn't see anything much except the boat, the stones under his feet, and the faint glow of the distant sun lighting the mist.

After securing the boat, Sebastian turned and quietly walked away from the rocky shore into the fog.

6

Raphael used his oar to hold off the dock to stop the boat from crunching into it. When they got close enough, he jumped off and grabbed the painter line that Briac tossed to him. The dock felt very ordinary. It didn't feel like something in the realm of Dream. It felt like solid plain wood under his feet. He tied the line to a cleat, and Anise and Briac climbed onto the wooden planks.

Raphael looked around, and his sense of ordinariness went away. The thick milky mist felt clammy and heavy, and the sun's light was just a faint yellow glow above them. You couldn't see more than a few feet in any direction. They were standing on a dock above the lake, but they could barely make out the water's surface.

"Anise," said Briac, "You've been here before. Where do we go?"

Anise shook her head. "We always just landed and started walking down the path." She pointed to a gravel paved way that could just be made out through the fog. It started from the edge of the last board of the dock. "After that, things got hazy. There were lots of conversations with master Callum in the mist. It seemed he could talk to everyone, alone, at the same time."

"The Keep?" said Briac.

"I never saw it," said Anise, "No one even mentioned it in class. Though, there were rumors that people used to know more about the Isle of the Wise than the current masters did."

"Well, I guess there's nothing for it, then," said Briac. He pulled the neck of his cloak a little tighter against the chill and started walking down the gravel path. Anise and Raphael followed. Anise felt a shiver run down her spine. The cold, dank mist felt unwelcoming.

7

They became quickly and wholly lost in the fog. There was nothing to be seen but the gravel path, the faint glow from the sun, and the omnipresent mist. The way twisted and turned, and it kept branching.

Raphael and Briac turned to Anise for guidance at the intersections. She had no better idea than they did, so she picked at random, trying to exude confidence to keep their spirits up. The cold, damp fog and the gloom were disheartening.

At first, they tried to track which way they turned at branches in the path, but there were too many splits. There was no way to record the turnings without a paper and quill. There were too many to remember.

There was no break in the mist. No sights to see other than an occasional scraggly bush or tree. It felt like they had walked for miles, though there was no way to tell if it was in circles or not. It occurred to Raphael at one point that if they had bits of colored cloth, they could mark trees, but they didn't have a supply of bits of colored cloth.

The lighting didn't change. Though it felt like it had been hours or even days, there was no way to tell how much time had passed. The fog smelled of moldy wood and faintly of the waters of the distant lake.

At one point, Iggy flew up into the mist. He scouted around a little, then landed again. "Burn," he said sadly as he shook his wrinkled gray head.

Eventually, Anise got annoyed. With no better idea which way was correct at the next intersection, she muttered irritably, "I'm a channeler. We're in Dream. By Luna's lips, this place should be mine." She lifted an arm to halt her companions and sat on the gravel in a cross-legged position.

Anise silently thanked the thick seat of her armor, which protected her from the cold and roughness of the path.

She sat quietly, eyes closed for a few minutes. Raphael and Briac waited, wondering what would happen next.

Anise opened her eyes and held out her arm. A black raven flapped its way through the fog, spread its wings wide to slow itself, and landed on her forearm, its talons digging into the thick material of her armor.

The raven cocked its head to one side, met Anise's gaze, and spoke in a voice between a raven's cawing and a person's speech.

"I wondered when you would get around to calling me."

8

Sebastian was even more lost than Anise, Briac, Raphael, and Iggy were. He had left the shore with not even the path they had to guide him. The opaque mist was more featureless without the gravel walkway. Now that he no longer had the splashing of the oars to distract him, the silence was deafening.

The fog was so dense that Sebastian had to move slowly. Each tree or bush sprang out of the mist suddenly, as he could only see a little way in front of him, and he had to ease his way forward so as not to hit something. The trees were little scraggly things. Hardly worth calling trees at all. Sebastian was no expert, but he didn't recognize what kind of trees they were.

He tried calling out once. He called, "Anise!" into the mist, though he had no idea if she was anywhere near the island. He only tried it once. His voice died in the fog, seemingly sucked out of the air by the vapor. He felt that it had been sucked out of his mouth, throat, and lungs as well.

Sebastian had no idea which way he was going. He tried to orient himself by the sun, but its faint glow overhead wasn't much use. It seemed as directionless as he was himself.

After a while, he fell into a slow, plodding pace. He started focusing on just the next step. The mist crept into his brain and made it hard to think of anything else. Then the next step forced his attention on itself. He stepped on something that crunched under his feet.

Sebastian looked down. He had stepped on a human bone. The bleached bones of a human skeleton littered the muddy ground beneath his feet. Sebastian backed off a step. He shook his head in disbelief. The bones had been there for a long time. He shivered. It wasn't just the cold. He thought this could be him if he didn't find his way.

He resumed walking. There was nothing he could do for whoever that had been. It made him sad that no one had been there to bury the body.

As earlier on the boat, he tried to maintain a straight course, but he had no idea if he was succeeding or not.

While he walked, he fell into reminiscing. There was nothing to do but think.

He remembered being the Knight of Moon & Shadow when he was younger. He thought about that time often and wasn't surprised that current events were bringing the memories back to him. Since then, he'd had lots of happy times, along with some sad ones, but nothing else even close to as magical had ever happened to him.

Sebastian thought of his visions of Luna. He sometimes contemplated the picture of the moon that the mayor had commissioned for his mantelpiece and wished that the likeness of Luna was better. He remembered how she had helped him on his quest. "Ah, Luna," he said quietly, "I wish you were here now."

The glow of sunlight in the mist above him started to move.

Sebastian started and looked up. He realized that it wasn't actually the sun's glow but, instead, another light coming toward him through the fog. At first, it seemed to be moving steadily toward him, then he saw that it was bobbing up and down as it came forward.

A light beam burst through the fog to hover in front of Sebastian. It bopped up and down as if on a string. A gleeful high-pitched voice broke through the murky silence.

"Hi," it peeped, "remember me? I'm Moonbeam."

9

Sebastian gaped at Moonbeam. As he had years ago when he first met the lunar sprite, he wondered how a little bouncing ball of light could talk. There was a shower of motes of brightness when it spoke, and it felt like its voice reverberated in the mist.

Sebastian shook his head. "Moonbeam," he said, "I thought you couldn't come out during the day?"

"Well, that's a fine how-do-you-do," said Moonbeam, "No greeting. No 'hello.' No Moonbeam, how are you? It's been forever? Just, 'I thought you couldn't come out during the day?'" The little spirit kept on, a cascade of flecks of light accompanying the flash of each sentence. "That's all right," it said, "You've got a lot to think about. Anyway, it's not really day. We're in Dream. Also, the fog keeps the sun away."

"I'm so sorry," said Sebastian. He meant it. "I'm thrilled to see you."

"That's all right," the little light wave repeated. "How did you get here, anyway?" It said. "This is Dream, and you're awake."

"I rowed a rowboat," said Sebastian. He glanced at the ripped handkerchief tied around his hands.

"That's an unusual way to get into a dream," said Moonbeam cheerily. The presence of the diminutive glow of light cut the gloom, and Sebastian felt hopeful. "Follow me," said the dab of moonlight, "Luna sent me to show you the way again." The light blob looked thoughtful, if such a thing is possible, and continued, "Did you ever think that you might have a bit of channeling power? You seem to have summoned me into your dream."

Without waiting for an answer, Moonbeam flashed off into the fog. Sebastian followed as quickly as he was able.

10

The raven perched on Anise's outstretched forearm, looking at them each in turn with its bright, intelligent eyes. Iggy launched himself into the air from Anise's other shoulder. He flew a circle around the group before landing on the ground. Anise got the idea that he was trying to show the raven that he was the winged member of the band.

Anise met the gaze of the raven's beady black eye. "Lord Morpheus?" she asked.

"Of course," said the bird. The raven spread his wings high and wide, still perched on her forearm, and cawed loudly. "Morpheus, Lord of Dream!"

Raphael's gaze got caught momentarily by the dark space under the raven's wings. He suddenly saw a flock of tiny winged people in the inky blackness. Then his gaze brushed past them, and he saw a green grassy field, a warm shining sun, and a place of peace and rest. For a moment, Raphael wanted nothing more than to dive into the welcoming space inside the blackness within the raven's feathers.

Lord Morpheus folded his wings. Raphael shook his head as if waking from a dream.

"Lord Morpheus," said Anise, "If you wouldn't mind. We could use some help getting through this mist."

"Anise," said the bird, "it is more than just the keeper of the underworld who stands to gain from your success. Mortals who rise above their stations can hurt us all." The bird launched himself into the air. His shadow fell over them as he rose above.

"Follow me," cawed the black bird. He started flapping onward above the path.

The companions followed the bird through twists,

turns, and intersections of the way. If he flew too fast and they lost him, he circled back until they could follow him again.

The gravel path ended in a clearing. The mist was thinner here, so the companions could see further. The outer wall of a keep rose before them on the other side of the open space. The stones of the keep had a greenish cast. They didn't look like anything seen in the waking world.

There were two massive doors in the wall. Side by side. They looked too thick and solid to be opened by any normal means. The raven landed in the center of the clearing.

"The Keep of Truth and Deceit," he cawed.

11

The stone walls of the keep towered overhead until they were lost in the mist high above. The doors weren't made of the same greenish stone as the rest of the wall. The one on the left was carved from the dark horn of some momentous beast. It glimmered translucently in the mist. The door on the right was polished ivory. It showed its shining surface as white as the milky fog, though it looked as solid as the stones that bordered it. Anise wondered what creatures could have been big enough to have grown the horns and the tusks. There didn't seem to be any seams or joints in the doors.

The raven lifted his head and fixed his beady eye again on the companions. "The Gate of Horn," he explained, "is the one I used to send forth dreams of fulfillment, dreams that brought the truth to the dreamer. He cocked his head to one side. "Though, truth be told, facts are sometimes more painful than fiction.

"The Gate of Ivory," said the raven, gesturing toward the right-hand door with his beak. "Is the door of deceit, lies, and fiction." The bird winked at Raphael. "It's what you saw under my wing," he said.

"There aren't any handles," said Anise, "Not even a knocker." She looked up toward the top of the doors. "And, they're so big."

"You need to decide which door to open," said the raven.

"I don't see how to open either one," said Anise, "And we don't need lies and deceit. I think it's obvious which door we should open."

"Is it?" said the raven. He cawed in a way that almost sounded like laughter, took to wing, and flapped off into the fog.

Anise pondered for a bit in the clammy mist. Briac's ability to click open a lock with a song wouldn't help when there weren't any locks. Raphael and Iggy didn't have any skills that she could think of to help here. And, anyway, she was pretty sure this was a job for a channeler.

Anise spent what felt like an eternity trying various magical tricks to open the Gate of Horn. Briac and Raphael helped by searching for mechanisms, seams, or anything that resembled keyholes, handles, or latches without success. Iggy helped by flying in random circles through the fog, calling out, "Burn," and occasionally splashing the door with a blast of flame.

In the end, it turned out to be simple. Anise, despairing of finding any way of getting the slightly translucent Horn Gate to budge, leaned lightly against the milky-white ivory one next to it. Smoothly and silently, the massive door swung inward. She turned to it and pushed a little more. It swung open wide enough for her and her companions to make their way through.

Anise shrugged and gestured for them to follow her as she walked through the Gate of Ivory into the Keep of Truth and Deceit.

12

Sebastian was trying his best to keep up with Moonbeam. It was hard as the lunar sprite flitted through the air freely, and he had to slog through the mire. The ground was marshy, and a thin layer of mud coated the soil.

It was the kind of mud that you don't sink into, but rather that attaches itself to the bottoms of your shoes. The type of mud that forms on the ground in a mist or after the first rainfall in a dry climate. With each step, a new thin layer would attach itself to the bottom of the previous layer. After a few steps, Sebastian felt like he was walking on raised platforms.

Stopping every few feet to knock the mud off his shoes didn't lead to high-speed travel. Moonbeam didn't seem to understand the trials of pedestrians, so Sebastian was very relieved when they crossed a gravel pathway.

"Moonbeam," he called out, "Can you lead us on a path that follows this walkway, please?"

The diminutive beam of moonlight darted back over to Sebastian. It looked at him. Though it is hard to say how it did that without eyes, a head, a neck, or any tangible physical manifestation.

"Of course," it chirped, "I'd be happy to." There was a brief pause. "Well, that is, I would love to," it continued. There was another brief pause. "I mean, I'd like to," it said. The showers of light that accompanied Moonbeam's speech were a bit dimmer with each sentence.

"I can't," Moonbeam pronounced. The little light trace sounded sad. "I don't know anything about the path. I just know which direction it is toward the Keep."

Sebastian sighed. He resigned himself to the mud. "That's all right, Moonbeam," he said. "Though maybe you could fly a little slower?"

It wasn't that much further. The mists opened up a little, though you still couldn't see the sun. Sebastian followed Moonbeam into the clearing in front of the Gates of Horn and Ivory.

13

Sebastian hardly noticed the gates. They were big and impressive, but they weren't what he was here for. He kicked the last mud off his shoes and walked past the doors to the right-hand side along the stone wall.

"A moment," warbled Moonbeam.

Sebastian stopped and turned to the beam of light.

"Uh-huh?" he said.

"I have to go," said Moonbeam sadly. "I didn't get to stay very long this time, did I?" The gleam of moonlight bopped up and down. "Maybe next time we could go on a whole adventure together?"

"Moonbeam," said Sebastian tearing up slightly, "Thank you so much."

The little light wave flitted up into the mist. As it had when it appeared, it looked like it was the circle of the sun showing through the fog before it disappeared, and the light returned to being directionless.

Sebastian started walking along the wall of the keep. The stones radiated a slight cold and reflected the light from the invisible sun, giving the mist an eerie green glow.

He followed the wall, seeing no break or gap in the stones. The moss-colored surface rose above him, preternaturally smooth, broken only by precise seams.

The first break in the uniformity was a line of low bushes growing just in front of the wall. Like the scraggly trees Sebastian had noticed while following Moonbeam, he didn't recognize the variety, but it didn't matter. *I'll call them "Dreamshrubs,"* he thought.

Sebastian pushed his way into the shrubs. Behind them was a low muddy ditch. There, low in the otherwise featureless green wall, was the Gate of Heroes. It was a small round hole in the wall, a culvert. A trickle of brownish water flowed through the gutter into the ditch, where it puddled in a pool of brown sludge.

Lying next to the hole in the ditch was a rusty metal grating. Jagged ends of metal stuck out of the culvert edges where it had been ripped off the wall. Sebastian wondered what kind of creatures would need a sewer in the Dream Realm.

Regretting what it would do to the white linen pants that Isabel had lovingly made for him, he got down on his knees. He carefully made his way over the sharp metal stubs of the broken grating.

Sebastian crawled through the Gate of Heroes into the Keep of Truth and Deceit.

THE KEEP OF TRUTH AND DECEIT

1

Anise stopped after stepping into the entrance hall of the keep. The hall was huge and had once been very elegant. A massive chandelier hung over the room's center, suspended by a thick chain glinting silver in the weak light. The others crowded in behind her. It was quiet and still in the vast space of the open hall.

Anise looked around. What little light there was, was seeping in from somewhere high above. Perhaps filtered by the green stone of the walls, similar to the exterior, the light cast an olive glow over everything in the hall. The lighting was dim enough that the far end of the room was lost in the distance.

The sides of the chamber were lined with chairs that were probably elegant once but were now moldering and falling apart. Tapestries concealed parts of the walls, ripped in places. Cobwebs lined the green surface, with a few web strands stretching from the tapestries to the chandelier. Some of the strands looked as thick as the lines tying up the boat they had used to cross the lake. Anise saw Raphael shiver as he inspected the webs. *He must be imagining the spiders that made them*, she thought.

High above the center of the room, the massive chandelier was formed from crystals that glinted emerald in the light. Above the dimly glittering gems were candles that looked like they had never been used. Anise wondered how anyone ever lit or replaced them. Then she remembered where she was.

Anise focused on the element of fire. It came easily. She only felt the presence of the Key of the Elements distantly, but a more nearby source of fire came surging into her. She remembered being unable to control the elements during her time in Dream. Still, this keep was somewhere between dreaming and waking. The candles burst into flame, flooding the hall with light.

The floor was emerald green, shiny, and polished. It reflected all the points of light from the candle flames above it. It appeared like it should feel slippery, but it didn't.

"Well," said Briac quietly into the silence of the vast hall, "if anyone didn't know that we are here, they know now."

2

Anise waited as the light from a hundred candles glittered and reflected off the facets of the emerald crystals and lit every corner of the vast open hall. She was stunned at her own audacity. Briac's quiet words faded into silence, and the stillness resumed.

No one came. There were no other sounds. Aside from Briac's comment, there was no response to the flood of light. Not even a scurrying sound implying that the spiders that made the cobwebs were still around.

After a moment of silence, Anise stepped forward, walked beneath the massive chandelier, and looked up at it. Briac trailed behind her. Raphael and Iggy moved off to the sides of the chamber. Raphael peered with interest at something on one of the tapestries. Iggy flitted up above the cobwebs. They shifted with the wind of his passing, and tiny dust flakes fell like snow.

Anise whispered to Briac, "A little bit flashy for Dream." She pointed upward. "Isn't the lord of dreams supposed to be somewhat subtle?"

"Why are you whispering?" said Briac, speaking in a voice barely louder than a whisper himself.

"It just feels like I should," whispered Anise, "to show some respect for what this place used to be."

"What did this place use to be?" said Briac.

"I have no idea," said Anise, a little bemused.

The light from the chandelier made more of the room visible. Corridors and side passages led out of the hall in various directions. Looking up above the chandelier, there were walkways connecting rooms on higher floors across the space of the chamber. Anise and Briac started walking under the chandelier, down the hall's center towards the far end.

They approached a large staircase leading upward. It was a beautiful curving stair made of the same green stone as the floor.

"Didn't the stories talk about going up?" said Anise.

"The things I read in the bard's library talked about the Lord of Dream being at the top of the keep," confirmed Briac.

"I bet that's where we'll find Lorenzo," said Anise determinedly. She put her foot on the first step of the staircase.

3

The glow from the fog-shrouded day behind Sebastian faded quickly. The faint light showed green walls with an arched stone ceiling above. The floor, wet with the trickle of brown water, was flat. There wasn't room to stand upright, but Sebastian could move forward slowly, half-crouched. He was grateful that he wasn't taller and thought, for once, that it would be nice to be shorter, as the crouch made him move very slowly. At some point, later on, he was sure there would be sore muscles.

Sebastian moved forward a few feet in his half-crouch and then stopped. The glow behind him was dim. The tunnel before him faded into blackness, especially with his body blocking some of the light. He thought about whether he had anything to help him see in the dark. He didn't have a lantern or a torch. He did have a flint and steel and a little bit of tinder, but that wasn't going to help by itself.

Sebastian wished that he had just a trace of Anise's facility with elements. He remembered her telling him something about a new element that produced light without heat. Sebastian wasn't sure how there could be a new element, but there was no arguing with Anise. She knew much more about this stuff than he did.

He could touch the tunnel's walls on both sides if he reached out, and the floor looked smooth enough, though his feet splashed in the muddy brown water. Sebastian sighed and reached out his arms to both sides. His fingertips barely brushed the tunnel walls. He crept forward into the blackness.

Sebastian moved very slowly, carefully putting first one foot out, then the other, before inching forward. After advancing into the darkness for what felt like a long time, he turned back and looked behind himself. The greenish glow of the culvert opening in the outside wall of the keep was distressingly close. He grunted, turned forward again, and tried to speed up his shuffling pace.

Soon enough, the darkness was complete. Sebastian's hearing became more acute now that he couldn't see. The noises of his own shuffling progress dominated. Still, he also heard the sounds of dripping water somewhere in the distance.

His fingers on the right-hand side lost contact with the wall. He tried to reach a little further and found an opening, a gap, in the wall on that side. Feeling around more, he discovered a branching tunnel, similar to the one he was in, going off to the right.

Sebastian had heard somewhere, he didn't remember where, that if you always followed one wall in a maze, you would eventually find your way through. Even though it meant that he would lose sight of the culvert's mouth behind him, he kept his hand on the right-hand wall and followed the side tunnel.

4

Sebastian was getting tired of the darkness. He had experienced it before, of course. Cloudy nights in the fields and his own bedroom's lightlessness after the candle had been blown out, but this was different. It didn't matter if he opened his eyes or closed them; the inky blackness was precisely the same.

He was making progress, he thought, though slowly. He kept his hand on the right-hand wall and turned to the right whenever there was a choice. Sometimes he walked upright through areas where the ceiling was higher. Sometimes there were multiple branches, and it was hard to even tell how many tunnels there were. He clung to the right-hand wall like it was a lover and hoped that Isabel wouldn't be jealous.

It felt like a puzzle why there were so many tunnels beneath the keep of the lord of dreams. Still, Sebastian had never been one to question the ways of the gods, and he wasn't about to start now.

His ears were working harder in the absence of his vision. After a while, he began to regret his newfound hearing sensitivity. At first, the sounds of his own limping progress and the occasional water drips were the only noises. Then he heard a scuttling, shuffling sound at the periphery of his hearing. It came and went. Sebastian was happy when it went. It sounded like something low to the ground clambering over the uneven surface of the tunnel floor. Sebastian felt a shiver run down his spine when he first heard it. It made him think of bugs or snakes.

He tripped over rough spots on the floor or fallen stones a few times. Each time he did, he slowed a little and tried to keep his forward movements deliberate and calm. It was hard when his instinct was to rush forward to get out of the crushing darkness.

Sebastian's relief when he saw a break in the blackness was enormous. At first, he didn't believe it. He thought it was a trick that his eyes were playing on him. He blinked and peered forward. There it was, a green glow straight ahead of him, a light gleaming in the distance. Trying not to hurry to the point where he tripped, Sebastian moved forward as quickly as possible.

5

Anise strode forward confidently without looking back, trying to give her companions the impression that she knew where she was going. The second floor of the keep was a tangle of corridors and rooms. Each doorway she opened felt like it would lead to someplace vital or unusual. Still, each, in its turn, was another disappointment.

She was looking for a staircase up. The assumption that the former lord of the keep had had his sanctuary at the top of the castle was the only thing she had to go on.

The rooms and corridors of the castle were opulent and lush, though they had fallen into disrepair. The walls were all of the same green stone. The floors all showed the same polished surface as the entrance hall, so there was no way to tell if someone had last passed by two minutes or two hundred years ago.

The rooms they walked by contained things that would have fascinated Anise at another time. Some of the rooms had open doors; some of them she opened herself. Either way, the rooms held things that might be mementos of pivotal or memorable dreams.

One room was full of instruments. There were all sorts of musical devices there. Briac's eye's opened wide. Anise shut the door again hurriedly.

She stopped in front of another door. There was a hissing sound from behind it. She glanced at Briac, who shook his head carefully. She opened the door a crack, then slammed it. The room beyond was crawling with snakes.

"I wonder what they eat," said Briac thoughtfully.

There was a room full of treasure. Gold coins, other golden objects, and shining gemstones. Anise tried to shield the view of what was in there from her companions. She closed that door hurriedly as well. *No sense tempting people*, she thought.

Anise opened one door that led into a huge kitchen. The counters and ovens were big enough for many cooks to work and for those cooks to provide food for many people. Or perhaps, other things. Anise thought she would have expected to see a kitchen on the ground floor. Then she reconsidered. The rules of the waking world didn't apply here in Dream.

She turned around and spoke, "Raffy," she said, "can you tell how recently someone has used this kitchen?" She noticed that Iggy's familiar weight was missing from her shoulder. There was no one behind her but Briac. He turned and looked behind himself, a slightly confused look on his face.

"Raffy?" Anise repeated.

6

Iggy flitted angrily through the air over Raphael's head. He looked like he was about to breathe a blast of fire. The fire imp had blasted the keep doors with flames when they had tried to get in. Raphael wondered if his improvised helmet would protect his head from the blaze.

"Burn!" said Iggy disdainfully.

Raphael thought for a minute; was it really disdainful? He scanned Iggy's expressionless face and tried to read the emotions behind the features. The big pupils in his catlike eyes were dilated because of the dim lighting. His gray leathery skin covered a face that otherwise looked almost human. Raphael wondered what it would take to get inside that head.

Iggy noticed Raphael looking at him and flapped slightly higher into the air. "Burn," he said again. It still sounded disdainful to Raphael.

"I didn't do anything," said Raphael. "It's as much your fault as mine that we're lost. You're the one who kept flying off down those corridors without looking to see which way they might have gone."

"Burn," conceded Iggy reluctantly.

Raphael looked around. They were at an intersection of several corridors. Off to one side was a staircase leading down. The walls were the same omnipresent green stone, and the floor shone like an emerald. They hadn't seen signs of any human presence since they lost track of Anise and Briac. Raphael had missed his companion's discussion of the lord's sanctuary being at the top of the keep.

"Come on, Iggy," he said with a cheerful facade. "Let's go down. The kitchens have to be on the lower levels, and that's where we'll find traces of life if there is anything to be found."

7

Iggy was flying low in front of Raphael. He was selecting which way they went, flitting forward quickly enough that Raphael had difficulty keeping up. Raphael was still trying to reason with him, though he wasn't sure it was worthwhile.

"Iggy," he called out, "It really wasn't my fault. I want to find them as much as you do."

"Burn," replied Iggy derisively. Raphael could tell from the lines of the muscles in the imp's back that he wasn't yet ready to forgive.

The kitchen Rafael had been looking for hadn't materialized. The walls of the corridors on this level were rougher and less finished than on the previous one. The seams between the stones weren't visible here. I wonder if these are tunnels, he thought. Maybe the whole island is made out of this green stone.

The lighting was dimmer. There were occasional openings high in the walls that let in a little faint greenish light. Raphael speculated that they were open to the floor above, expressly to be light tunnels. Still, between the light-tunnel mouths, the corridors were poorly lit.

At one point, Raphael stumbled in the gloom. Iggy turned back, glared at him, and hissed slightly. He turned again and flew forward, but his body started to glow with a muted fiery red glow. Though ruddy and contrasting oddly with the green walls, the illumination was enough to see by.

Iggy kept flitting forward. He flew down corridors, through rooms, and across green-lit murky spaces, hardly looking around. Raphael thought that the fire imp's only focus was seeing Anise's familiar black-clad form again.

"Iggy," called out Raphael again, "We should slow down

and look where we're going."

Iggy flew through an ornate wide-open double doorway into a large room, with Raphael right on his heels. The heavy doors, made of the same green stone as the walls and floor, slammed shut behind them with a thunderous crash.

A spectral voice boomed out, "Die intruders! Thou shalt not pass!" as a tall skeletal figure stepped out into the middle of the room and lifted a gleaming silvery sword into the air.

8

As Sebastian headed toward the glimmering green light in the distance, it got brighter. It didn't become any less green, but with the color of the stone walls of the keep, Sebastian wasn't too surprised at that. What did surprise him a little was how the scuttling shuffling sound he had been hearing got louder as he approached the light. What surprised him more was how the glow started moving as he got closer.

It separated out into multiple tiny green points of light. They were moving in some kind of haphazard way. Then, on second thought, Sebastian realized that it wasn't entirely random. He felt like there was some kind of connection between the sounds and the motion of the lights.

Sebastian stopped his inching forward. He looked more carefully, trying to make out what he was seeing. A drop of condensation from the tunnel rocks overhead dropped off and landed in his eye. He wiped his face and peered ahead. The green glow outlined a tunnel mouth into a larger lit chamber, regardless of anything else. He started forward again. The prospect of being able to see outweighed any hesitations.

He was almost at the tunnel mouth before he could make sense of what his vision was telling him. The green lights were dancing around in an oval pattern. The motion of the lights was accompanied by the scuttling sound he had been hearing. The end of the tunnel opened out into a larger chamber, with the skittering lights toward the middle.

What made Sebastian's heart beat a little faster was what he saw above the green lights in the chamber's ceiling. There were three round holes with faint glows of light coming from them. It might be filtered, faint daylight, unlike the glowing dots below it.

He stepped to the threshold of the tunnel mouth. There

was a bit of a knocking sound as his foot bumped against an unseen rock on the tunnel floor. The moving green dots stopped.

In the center of the room, with all their bulbous eye stalks turned toward Sebastian, was a circle of green crablike creatures. Each was the size of a large cat or a small dog and had a third sinewy stalk behind their eye-stalks from which hung suspended the green glowing orbs of light that Sebastian had been seeing. The bodies of the crabs were barely visible in the green glows they were producing themselves.

They had been dancing in a circle in the middle of the room. With Sebastian's entrance, they all turned in his direction. The silence was momentarily absolute before the skittering sound resumed as they all started scuttling toward him.

9

Sebastian reached for his sword. He still had the ripped half of his handkerchief wrapped around his palm, and he felt the rowing blisters as he pulled the sword from its sheath. He stepped a little further into the room to give himself space to stand upright and swing the sword if he needed to.

Sebastian was pretty sure he would need to. The crablike creatures were all scurrying toward him distressingly fast. The ones nearest to him raised their claws into the air. They started clicking them open and closed. The clicking sound joined the scrabbling sound of their motion to fill the air with noises that made the hairs on the back of Sebastian's neck rise.

He glanced around to get the lay of the land. The three holes in the ceiling were filtering in a little bit of a slightly healthier-looking light. Beneath each hole, in the room's center where the crabs had gathered, was a mound of mossy earth. The room was damp. Water rivulets ran across the floor from multiple tunnel mouths that looked similar to the one behind Sebastian.

There had to be at least twenty of the creatures scuttling toward him. Still, in his inspection of the room, Sebastian saw something that gave him some hope. On one wall of the room, he saw a rusty iron ladder. The bars looked aged, but they might hold his weight, and he imagined that the crabs wouldn't be able to climb the ladder.

The first of the crabs reached him. Sebastian took up a fencing pose like his father had taught him, though he knew this would be a very different fight than a fencing bout. He thrust his sword at first one of the crabs, then the next, trying to get them to stay a little distance away from his legs.

The sword bounced off the tough shell of a crab. They started to surround him. He felt a pinch as a claw closed on the

back of his leg through the thick linen of the white britches
Isabel and Anise had made for him years ago.

10

Anise gawked at Briac. "Where are they?" she said. "When was the last time you saw them?" They stood in the kitchen doorway, the large room with its ovens, counters, and food storage cabinets on one side and the corridor they had come down on the other.

"I don't know," said Briac. "Was I in charge of Raphael?" He looked around again, "and, who do you mean by them?" He noticed Anise's shoulder. "Oh, Iggy's gone, too," he concluded.

"We have to go find them," said Anise, a note of panic sounding in her voice.

"I have no more idea how to find them than I do to find where we're going," said Briac.

"We could backtrack," said Anise.

"We could try," said Briac.

They made their way through the halls and corridors, trying to retrace their steps. There were countless rooms and hallways, and something about the layout of the passages was confusing. Walking through, trying to find where they had come from, reminded Briac of a distant, almost forgotten dream. When they came to a staircase leading upward rather than the one they had climbed from the floor below, even Anise had to admit that retracing their steps wasn't working.

"They can't be in any danger," said Briac. "There hasn't been a sign of life in the whole place so far."

"I'm still worried," said Anise.

"You know what," said Briac. "We're the ones going to deal with Lorenzo. He's the danger in this place. I bet they're a lot safer where they are than they would be with us."

Anise looked thoughtful. "Maybe you're right. Maybe they're safer not being in the confrontation with Lorenzo."

Briac nodded. "What use was Raphael going to be

anyway, with his kitchen cleaver and his pot on his head."

Anise gave him a scowl before starting up the stair.

11

Iggy flapped his wings backward and flopped down on Raphael's shoulder. He made a little deflated hissing noise, whispered, "Burn," and faded into smoke. With the part of his brain that wasn't occupied with the tall sword-wielding figure standing before him, Raphael noticed that Iggy's weight lessened noticeably when he faded. *That's how Anise has been able to carry him for so long*, Raphael thought.

The figure standing in the middle of the room was impressive. It looked like it had once been a tall armored man, but it was now an armored, animated skeleton. Bits of rotting flesh dropped off its grinning skull and off the parts of its bones that could be seen under its armor. It wore a shirt and leggings of chain mail that must have fit tightly when it had flesh on its bones. Now they draped over the skeletal remains. A moldy faded red cloth tabard covered its chest. A black silhouette of a dragon's head was on the tabard on the place where the figure might once have had a heart.

"Which is it?" said Raphael.

The skeleton lifted its sword and took a step toward Raphael. "Huh?" it said. Raphael looked with interest at how its jaw moved as it spoke. *It doesn't have a throat, lips, or a tongue*, he thought, *so how is it speaking?*

"'Die intruders,' or 'Thou shalt not pass,'" said Raphael, "They're kind of incompatible." He pulled his cleaver out of its improvised sheath. "If you're going to kill us," he said, "then the 'Thou shalt not pass' part is redundant. If you're just going to stop us from passing, that doesn't involve killing us, necessarily."

"Shut up," said the skeleton eloquently. It struck out with its sword. The blade glinted in the olive light.

The blow was horizontal. Raphael ducked to try to evade

it and, at the same time, knocked the blade upward with his cleaver. It clanged off his helmet as he barely ducked under the stroke.

I wish Briac was here, thought Rafael. *He wouldn't be laughing at my helmet now.*

12

Iggy faded into solidity on Raphael's shoulder and launched himself into the air. The sudden change in weight and the motion startled Raphael, and he dropped his cleaver. Fortunately, the skeletal guard was also surprised. It fell to one knee, lifted its sword in front of itself, and cried, "Dragon," in a voice that almost sounded excited.

Iggy flared bright red as he blasted a burst of flame at the guard.

A wave of fire bathed the figure. Raphael scrambled to retrieve his cleaver. The faded red tabard started burning, and the chain mail glowed with heat. Iggy flitted back to Raphael and settled onto his shoulder. The skeletal figure rose and advanced on Raphael again, parts of its body flaming. It didn't seem to be hindered by the fire.

"Doesn't that hurt?" said Raphael.

"No," said the skeletal figure. Raphael thought he detected a note of sadness in its voice.

"By the way," said Raphael, "Iggy's not a dragon. He's a fire imp."

The flaming skeleton looked more intimidating than it had before. The tabard was blazing, and even some of the skeleton's flesh seemed to be burning. Waves of heat came from it.

"Maybe, don't try that again," said Raphael in an aside to Iggy. Raphael scrutinized the burning undead figure before him. It occurred to him that this had once been a man. Something had happened to him to make him into this fearful creature. "What's your name?" said Raphael to the flaming skeleton.

"Why would you care?" said the skeletal guard. It thrust forward with its sword.

Raphael noticed the sword again; it seemed polished and well maintained. It didn't match the rest of the guard's aged equipment. He also observed, with relief, that the guard was attacking relatively slowly. He was able to jump out of the way of the thrust.

"Well," said Raphael, "I can't just keep thinking of you as the skeleton or the skeletal guard. That's not very nice."

"My name was Edward," said the skeleton. "Edward of the Ashton Dragon's Watch. My friends called me Ed." It started another swing with its gleaming sword. "You won't have to call me anything for long, but you can call me Ed."

Raphael stepped backward while wielding his cleaver to deflect the blow. "Ed? Does that mean we're friends?" he said.

"No," said Edward.

THE ROOM OF DOORS

1

Anise and Briac reached the top of a staircase. The open space at the top formed a room, which, like the entrance hall, was lined with mildewed, upholstered chairs. At the end of the hall was a broad set of double doors. They stood open, showing another large room behind them. Master Lorenzo was standing in the door frame, leaning casually against one of the side jambs.

Briac reached for the dagger on his belt. Anise dropped into a fighting crouch, pulling her spear off her back and wishing her shield into existence on her left arm. She cleared her mind for quick access to the elements.

It was a younger Lorenzo than Anise had ever met. He reminded her of Sebastian's descriptions of the hearty man he had met on his journey as the Knight of Moon and Shadow years ago. He even had the handlebar mustache that her uncle had told her about. It drew the eye like a magnet. The handles reached out on each side, forming intricate spirals. The spirals of waxed hair bobbed up and down when Lorenzo moved. They shone in the dim light and almost seemed to spin around.

Ignoring Briac and Anise's reaction to his presence, Lorenzo stepped forward and opened his arms as if expecting a hug. "Anise," he called out in a robust youthful voice, "it's so good to see you again. I've been waiting for you." He took in Briac's presence and smiled a warm smile that made it hard not to smile back. "And, who is this handsome young man?"

"Lorenzo," hissed Anise, but she already had the feeling that this wasn't going the way she had expected it to.

"Anise," said Lorenzo, sounding like the purest voice of reason, "Let's keep this civilized." He gestured into the room behind himself, "I've set up a table; why don't we sit down and have a cup of tea."

Briac leaned over and whispered into Anise's ear, "Careful, I think this is a trap."

"Of course it is," Anise whispered back. To Lorenzo, she said, "Civilized? You tried to kill me. You trapped me in the realm of Dream for fifteen years. You tried to kill my uncle. Your actions are endangering the world. They're endangering not just one world, but two."

"That doesn't mean we can't enjoy a spot of tea and maybe some biscuits," said Lorenzo, "You must be starving."

2

Anise and Briac followed Lorenzo through the double doors. As they stepped into the room, Anise realized that she'd been there before. It was the Room of Doors from her experimentation with clairvoyance.

The room was just as impressive as it had been in her meditative dream state. The doors, each unique, were strewn over the walls and floor. The large stone pool she had noticed before was not that far away. The back wall of the room was lost in the distance. The ceiling still showed a swirling mist. Anise felt a bit of a chilly wind blowing down from above. There was a startlingly ordinary dining table surrounded by several chairs near the entrance.

Her mouth dropped open. "But this room is in Dream, or clairvoyance, or something," she said.

"Of course it is," said Lorenzo. "As are we."

Anise looked over the contents of the table. There was a pot of tea and a selection of cookies and cakes. She almost drooled. She realized that they hadn't eaten anything since coming to Isle of the Wise.

"So," she said, "What's poisoned?"

Lorenzo looked hurt. "Anise," he said, "You think me that unoriginal? I said that we'd keep this civilized. That didn't work on your uncle, and of course, it won't work on you. You are Academy trained, after all. I remember Master Ernst's lessons on sniffing out poisons as if it were yesterday."

It was true. Anise could tell that there wasn't any poison in the foodstuffs on the table. She took a seat, grabbed a piece of cake like it was a lifeline thrown to a drowning person, and nodded at Briac. He sat as well.

Master Lorenzo took a chair at the head of the table. He watched Anise and Briac eat for a moment, then poured out three cups of tea. He nodded with thought. The spirals on his mustache bobbed up and down intriguingly. "So," he said, "we've got a lot to talk about. Let's talk."

3

Sebastian kept thrusting at the crabs, trying to keep them at bay, but there were too many. He felt the nips and pinches of them clawing at his legs. The thick white linen of his britches was being shredded. He had a moment of regret as he thought about how lovingly Isabel and Anise had crafted them for him. Then it occurred to him that there would be more regrets if he didn't manage to change the situation. Or perhaps he wouldn't have anything to regret anymore at all.

He changed his point of attack. Instead of thrusting his sword at the hard-shelled bodies of the crabs, he swung his sword at the third eye-stalk of the nearest, feeling like a boy swiping a stick at a dandelion stem.

His sword struck true. The crab's eye-stalk cut easily, and half of it, topped by the glowing green orb, fell to the ground. There was a high-pitched keening sound, and the crab scuttled off toward the mounds of earth in the center of the room. The rest of the creatures paused. The green orb on the end of the fallen stalk continued to glow for a moment before it started to fade.

Sebastian pressed his momentary advantage. He sprang forward, landing on top of the broad shell of a crab before jumping off, reaching out, and grasping one of the rungs of the rusty iron ladder.

Sebastian climbed quickly, trying to get his legs out of range of the crab's claws. The creatures scuttled forward to crowd around the ladder's base, snapping their claws at his retreating legs in frustration.

The top of the ladder ended at the room's ceiling and a trapdoor, locked with a rusty iron padlock. Sebastian pushed at the door and scrabbled at the padlock, but neither gave way. His legs felt weak. He didn't know how long they would hold him, between the exertion and the cuts and bruises they had taken from the crab's claws. The crabs beneath the ladder seemed to know this. They snapped their claws, making an ominous din.

Sorry father, thought Sebastian. He took his sword and pressed the tip into the padlock's shackle. The rusty iron gave way before the hardened steel. There was a crack as the metal broke.

Sebastian pushed open the trapdoor, climbed the last few rungs, his legs trembling, and dropped to the floor of the room above.

4

It took Sebastian several minutes before he could do anything but try to catch his breath. The pain of his cuts and bruises intruded into his attention. He sat up, scanned the room briefly, then inspected his legs to assess the damage.

The lighting was better here, though the green walls made the space feel eerie and tainted. The trapdoor had led into a garderobe. A bench with three seats with round holes in the middle was built into one wall. A door stood open against the other. Sebastian estimated that the holes were right over the three mounds of soil below.

His pants were a total loss. The white linen was shredded and torn. Under it, his legs, though tired and painfully scraped and bruised, were not as seriously injured as he had thought they would be. It reminded him of the line from the old folk song that wandering minstrels sometimes sang when they visited Hero. One of the final lines in the song "Fiona and Irene" was, "The two girls sprawled together, scrapes and bruises, that was all."

Now that the immediate danger was past, Sebastian's mind was left flooded with thoughts by the receding adrenaline. He thought about how sad it was that his pants, though not the original Pants of the Wind, were left in this disheveled state. He thought about how innovative the idea of a garderobe over flowing water was. There had probably been more water flowing in the tunnels below at one time. With the water washing away the waste, you could use the garderobe without encountering unpleasant odors.

Sebastian shook his head. He didn't have time for these thoughts. He had to try to find Lorenzo to confront him.

He opened his backpack, trying to remember what Lilith had told him about the potions and vials she had given him. Sebastian selected a vial with a red ribbon tied around the stopper, opened it, and swallowed the contents. He felt a surge of energy and a bit of relief from the pain in his legs.

He remembered Maeve's story. The Lord of Dream had been in a room on the top floor of the Keep. He had to find his way up.

Sebastian rose to his feet. He felt the air moving around his legs through the rips and tears in the linen. *They're once again the Pants of the Wind*, Sebastian thought. He shook his legs a few times to shake the wobble out of them and left the garderobe to find a staircase leading upward.

5

Raphael held up his cleaver to ward off another blow from Edward's gleaming silvery sword. Iggy faded back and forth between smoke and solidity on his shoulder. He seemed to be trying to think about what he could do to help. Raphael was getting used to the weight change.

"I'm not actually an intruder," said Raphael. "I'm just lost. I wandered in here by mistake."

"That doesn't make you any less of an intruder," said Edward. He struck a bit of a pose, his gleaming sword held high. He did look impressive, between the silvery blade and his flaming red tunic. "I've been on guard here for two hundred years. No one has gotten past me in all that time."

"So, Edward from the Ashton Dragon's Watch," said Raphael, "Ed. Two hundred years? That's a long time. What are you guarding? Have many people tried to get past you? How did you become an undead skeleton living beneath the Keep of Truth and Deceit?"

"You talk too much," said Edward. He firmed his grip on his sword. Raphael glanced at the skeleton guard's hand.

"How do you hold your sword without any meat on your fingerbones?" he asked. Raphael wondered if that might be part of why the skeleton was wielding his sword slower than he might have been.

"It was hard at first," said Edward. "I had to adjust my grip."

"Ed," said Raphael reasonably, "didn't your mother tell you that you should be polite to strangers? I think you should answer some of my questions. What are you guarding, and who left you here?"

Edward grinned. Though, with a bare, flaming skull for a face, he didn't really have any other facial expressions available to him. "Don't you talk about my mother," he said, swinging his sword a little more fiercely this time, "She was a saint."

Raphael pressed his advantage while evading Edward's sword. "So, she did," he said. "She told you to be polite to strangers and that you should answer questions, didn't she?"

6

Edward's jaw moved in his grinning face. Raphael wondered how much the voice he perceived when Edward spoke sounded like Edward had when he was alive. Though, if he'd heard a living person talk in the same spectral, haunted voice Edward used, he would immediately have run away.

"It was the masters from the Academy," said Edward. Raphael kept quiet; it felt like a dam was about to burst. "The masters from the Academy," continued Edward. "They asked for a volunteer. They wanted someone who wasn't married. They wanted someone who felt that the mission of the Dragon's Watch was more important to them than their life."

"And, that was you," said Raphael.

"That was me," said Edward. Something about his voice sounded sad to Raphael. Though it still had the same mournful unearthly quality of infinite agony that it always had, there seemed to be an element of human grief in there as well.

"That must have been hard," said Raphael sympathetically. "Being stuck down here all alone." He clucked his tongue. "Wasn't there anyone you missed? Anyone you left behind?"

"There was a girl," said Edward. "It was hard to say goodbye." Edward thrust again with his sword, though it seemed that his heart, or whatever was under that part of his smoldering tabard, wasn't in it.

Raphael easily parried Edward's halfhearted thrust. "Did they tell you what you were to guard?" he asked.

"Of course," said Edward. He pointed to the far wall. There was a table against the wall behind the skeleton. On the table was a silver bowl containing a glowing blue crystal. The table, bowl, and crystal looked less aged than the other furnishings, though nothing in that room could be said to look unworn with time.

"What is it?" said Raphael.

"I don't know, exactly," said Edward. "Some kind of magical ward, I guess. I did speak to a clairvoyant before I left Ashton for the last time. She said if it was ever broken, it would 'open the path for the allies of Death's Daughter.' That sounds like a bad thing, don't you think?"

"It does sound bad," said Raphael, thinking the opposite.

7

R aphael nodded sympathetically at Edward. They had moved to a stage in their duel where it was almost more a dance than a fight. Edward would make a lackluster attack, and Raphael would make whatever minimal effort was needed to make it look like it had threatened him. The dance steps moved back and forth.

"You must be really bored," Raphael said feelingly. "And tired."

"Chronos' crusty codpiece!" said Edward. "I'm so bored! You're the first person to come here in two hundred years!" He shook his head from side to side. Bits of burning mummified skin flew off. "For the first fifty years, my sword would talk to me, but we ran out of things to say."

Raphael tried to look Edward in the eyes. It was difficult, as there were just two sunken black holes where they should have been. "My name is Raphael," said Raphael, "But you can call me Raffy." He smiled to himself as if at an inside joke. "If you do, you'll be one of only two people who call me that."

"I'm honored," said Edward. Raphael couldn't tell if he was being sarcastic or not.

Iggy sat on Raphael's shoulder, calmly watching the back and forth of sword, cleaver, and words. He seemed to have accepted both his perch and the non-threatening nature of the duel.

"Your job," said Raphael thoughtfully as he dodged Edward's latest thrust, "It's not very good, is it?"

"I have good job security," said Edward loyally.

"No breaks, no time off, no vacation, no pay," said Raphael. "You don't even know if this thing," he nodded toward the crystal, "still means anything anymore."

Edward stopped moving. His arm, holding his gleaming

sword, lowered to his side. "I'm really tired," he said.

"You know," said Raphael, "you've earned a rest. Two hundred years is a long time."

"You know," said Edward sadly, "It is."

8

Lorenzo leaned forward from his seat at the end of the table. He nodded to Briac and then looked Anise in the eye. "Anise," he said, "I know we've put the wrong foot forward first, but I think we can resolve this. I think I have some points to make to help you see things from my perspective."

Anise stared back at Lorenzo. Now that her hunger wasn't driving her anymore, she felt her rage returning. "Lorenzo," she said, "there is nothing you can say that will change the facts. You are wrong. You are wrong about many things. Your methods are wrong, and your goals are wrong. The use of clairvoyance is shattering the border between reality and dream, and you've misunderstood the prophecies that you follow so blindly."

Lorenzo leaned back in his chair. He stroked his mustache. It was hard not to follow his finger's path as it wove its way around the spiral and through the glistening curves.

"Anise," he said, "and you too, son," with a nod to Briac, "Let me try to explain." He gestured to the room behind him, to the doors and the stone basin on the floor. Anise noticed for the first time that the metal cover that had been closing the pool the last time she had seen it was hanging open.

"We need this power," said Lorenzo, "We need to know what's coming. With the power of clairvoyance, and especially now that I've managed to open the Scrying Pool, we will have the ability to predict dangers and disasters that threaten Liamec." His finger kept moving around the spiral of his mustache. Anise found it hard not to follow it with her eyes.

"I'm proud of what I've accomplished here," continued Lorenzo. "I've single-handedly brought clairvoyance back to the Academy. I've found this place and managed to open the

Scrying Pool. I've brought clairvoyance, a tool that Liamec vitally needs, back to us. I've been gathering power. Being head of the channeling department is just the first step. Soon I'll be headmaster of the Academy." The spirals on the ends of Lorenzo's mustache seemed to be spinning in Anise's mind. It was hard to keep her eyes open.

Lorenzo frowned. "The only thing I've failed at, so far," he said, "is you." His frown deepened. "I've been softhearted. I need to be tougher. There are no means that my ends don't justify."

Anise felt sorry for Lorenzo. *Why was she making things so difficult for him? He was only trying to do what was right.* With half her attention, she managed to sneak a glimpse at Briac. He was slumped in his chair, his eyes riveted on Lorenzo's mustache. A line of drool descended from one corner of his mouth to somewhere near his belt.

9

Anise shook herself. She sat upright and glared at Lorenzo. "That wasn't very nice," she said. She leaned over and slapped Briac across the face. He started, sat up straighter himself, and wiped the line of drool off his mouth. He looked confused.

"I'm sorry, Anise," said Lorenzo. He leaned back in his chair. The swirls on his mustache stopped spinning. "I was pretty sure that wouldn't work, but I had to try." He grinned ruefully. "It worked a little better than I thought it would."

Anise frowned. She pushed her chair back from the table and stood up. She readied herself to connect with the elements to prepare for a fight.

"Lorenzo," she said, "You have to yield. I don't want this to turn physical, but I am prepared to kill you if I have to. I have it on the best authority that you are wrong about the prophecies you have been following. The dark channeler named in the prophecies is you, not me. You're the one who is leading the world toward its doom. You're the one who is cracking reality. The use of clairvoyance and this scrying pool will destroy everything if I don't stop you."

Lorenzo looked confused, like what Anise said was getting through to him. Then, his confident, assured expression reappeared, and he replied, "I know what needs to be done. I'm the only one who knows. We can use the clairvoyants and the scrying pool to fix any problem. We have to use the power we have to fix this, to solve this."

"The solution is to stop using the power," said Anise. "The dream storms are going to get worse until reality fractures. One of the dragons told me …,"

Lorenzo laughed. "The dragons. They don't know anything. You know, clairvoyance was dropped from the

Academy curriculum because they were attacking Ashton? They have some kind of folktale about this and are obsessed with stopping it. The Academy masters two hundred years ago warded this Keep against them. They can't come here. They won't be a problem."

10

Edward sat in one of the dusty, faded, upholstered chairs lining the room's walls. He laid his sword on his lap. It gleamed silver. Raphael noticed again how shiny the blade was. The skeleton guard looked like he would have sighed if he'd still had lungs.

Iggy faded into visibility, flew off Raphael's shoulder, landed on the ground, and started peering around the room. Edward hardly spared him a glance.

"Raphael," said the skeletal guard. His voice sounded plaintive. "Do you think I could rest for a bit?" The remaining scraps of his tabard had stopped burning. Only part of the black dragon silhouette on his chest was still detectable.

"Ed," said Raphael, "The masters who recruited you must be dead now. The Keep has been abandoned for hundreds of years. I think you can rest as long and as deeply as you want."

Ed settled back in his chair. His bones seemed to lose some tension. "I'm so tired," he said, "I think I'll just close my eyes for a moment."

Raphael stepped over closer to the skeleton. He rested his hand on Ed's chain mail-clad shoulder. The metal links still felt warm under his hand from the fire. He could feel Ed's shoulder bone through the mail.

"Raffy?" said Ed.

"Yes, Ed?"

"Take my sword when I'm gone," the skeleton's voice grew faint. "She's a good sword. One of the masters at the academy made her for me. Take care of her. We haven't talked in a while, but tell her I forgive her."

"I will," said Raphael.

The skeleton guard settled a little further into his chair, and something seemed to leave him.

"You rest now, Ed," said Raphael. "You have a good, peaceful rest."

Raphael stood a moment with his hand on the cooling chain mail. Then he picked up the gleaming silvery sword, strapped it to his belt, and walked over to the table with its bowl and the blue crystal.

Open the path for the allies of Death's Daughter, he thought. *That's what I'm here to do, isn't it?* Iggy flitted over and landed on Raphael's shoulder again. Raphael raised his cleaver and brought it down on the glowing blue crystal, shattering both the crystal and the sharp steel blade into splinters.

11

Anise and Lorenzo faced off near the table. Briac was still sitting in his seat, looking confused, as he tried to shake Lorenzo's control off his mind. The academy-trained mages looked ready to tap into the elements to attack each other. Still, they were trying final attempts to sway things with words.

"Anise," said Lorenzo, "We can't let this opportunity go. We have to use the power this Keep, clairvoyance, and the scrying pool give us."

"Lorenzo," replied Anise, "you have all these clairvoyants telling you the future. You must have seen the coming destruction. You must have seen that the dream storms will get worse."

"They get worse, and the world ends if the dark channeler wins. If you win. The storms get worse if I fail in my endeavors." Lorenzo smiled. He looked almost giddy, almost drunk. "Anise, you have to see it," he gestured toward the stone basin. "The fluid in the Scrying Pool, it's raw dream stuff. It glows with the power of Dream. The clairvoyants gaze into the pool when they pass through here onto their paths, and their visions become even more powerful. It's beautiful. Just looking at it makes you feel that you can control the future."

As Anise glanced at the pool, she could see the contents. It was a seething mass of green fluid. It looked the same color as the stone walls of the Keep. She felt it calling to her; she felt its power. It was beguiling. It was also bubbling fiercely like a pot about to boil over.

There was a noise like the crack of a sail opening, and a wind came down from above. Anise and Lorenzo both turned to look up. A vast dark shape appeared above the open roof of the Room of Doors. Even though there was no apparent direct light source, a shadow flew chillingly across them.

A massive dragon crashed to the floor between Lorenzo and the wide double doors into the rest of the Keep. It reared back, spread its wings, and roared furiously. The greens stones of the Keep shook.

12

The dragon towered over Lorenzo. Anise recognized her; it was Flambé. She had gotten huge. They couldn't see the open double doors behind her with her wings spread. Her roar still reverberated through the hall. The wind from her flapping wings made it hard to stand.

Lorenzo stood unintimidated, not giving any ground. He began readying his elemental magics.

Anise realized that she had no clue about the life cycle of dragons. She had no idea how old Flambé would have been when she was in the menagerie at the Carnival of Wonders, and she had no idea if this was Flambé full-grown or not.

A voice rang out in Anise and Lorenzo's minds. Like on the previous occasions when Flambé had spoken to Anise, she didn't use sound but somehow communicated to them directly. Briac, sheltering behind the table, didn't seem to know that the dragon was speaking.

Dark channeler, Flambé said, *Your time has come. Your plans are failing you now.*

Lorenzo looked curious. Anise found it hard not to admire his fortitude faced with the creature in front of him. "How did you get in, beast?" he said. "The wards on this place keep your kind out."

Flambé roared again and stamped one of her mighty feet. The stones shook once more. *Your wards are down dark one. There is nothing for you to hide behind.*

"Those wards have stood strong for two hundred years," said Lorenzo. "I'm not sure how you have brought them down. When I last checked, the guardian still stood, and the crystal was untouched."

I have done nothing, wizard, said Flambé. *Your protections have fallen by themselves.*

Lorenzo frowned. "Well," he continued, as he prepared himself once again to summon the elements, "If it's a fight you want ...,"

The dragon was about to launch herself toward the channeler when they were interrupted from an unexpected direction.

"Anise!" called a familiar voice from behind the vast creature.

13

As Flambé whirled around blindingly fast, Anise saw a single human-sized figure standing behind the dragon's black-scaled body in the double doorway. The figure was dwarfed by the dragon.

Anise had a flashback to twenty years ago. It was the knight of Moon & Shadow. Sebastian stood there, his sword in hand, his legs trembling with weariness. He wore his purple thistledown jerkin, though the color had faded with time until it was more pink than purple. His white leggings were tattered and torn. Anise felt her heart go out to her knight, her uncle, whom she hadn't seen except in Dream in years.

Moving faster than Sebastian or Anise thought possible, the dragon launched herself at this new threat, this ambush from behind. She grabbed Sebastian around the midriff in her jaws, lifted him into the air, shook him, and threw his limp body aside into the corner of the room. His sword clattered to the ground. Tufts of thistledown from inside his jacket and little scraps of purple linen drifted through the air.

"Uncle Sebastian!" cried out Anise. She started to run toward the limp figure.

Flambé began to turn back toward Lorenzo, then gagged, coughing and choking like she had eaten something that really didn't agree with her.

Lorenzo took advantage of the confusion and began to summon the winds. "I'm sorry about your uncle, Anise," he said. "You know, I always liked him, even all things considered." He lifted both arms high, swinging them toward the dragon. "But, his distraction has given me time to do this." A mighty wind rose, building as it flew toward Flambé. The dragon was still coughing and spitting.

Anise was on her way toward the limp body in the

corner. Briac sprinted from his position behind the table and intercepted her. "Anise," he said, "let me check on your uncle." He pointed behind them. "I really think you need to take care of that."

The hurricane Lorenzo had raised had lifted Flambé's massive body off the green floor. She was being held spreadeagled against the wall by the immense focused wind. While holding the dragon immobile with the gale, Lorenzo used his control of the earth to pry loose a decorative iron bar from a door frame. The bar had a wrought iron spearhead on one end.

With a crack, the iron bar broke loose. The bar, with its spearhead, started shooting through the air directly toward the pinioned dragon's exposed breast.

14

Anise cried out, "No!" as she directed her own stream of air across the mighty wind blowing from Lorenzo toward the dragon. She had had less time to prepare, so her gust was a lesser force than the gale flowing from the older mage, and she didn't have time to directly work with the metal spear. Still, the wind was enough to shift the wrought iron bar with its decorative spearhead slightly to the side. Instead of piercing the dragon's breast, the metal cut a hole in her pinioned wing before rebounding off the green stone and clattering to the ground.

Anise's gust also had the effect of lessening the force of the gale holding the dragon to the wall. She dropped to the floor.

Flambé spat one more time to clear her mouth and throat of some bitter taste and launched herself into the air.

Anise took a moment to glance over at Briac in the corner. He was hovering over Sebastian's crumpled body. She couldn't tell anything more about what was happening there.

Lorenzo looked taken aback at the failure of his cast spear. His nonchalance was broken. He splayed his fingers and launched a set of blazing bolts of fire toward the onrushing dragon.

Anise felt the wind grow chill around them as Lorenzo's fire sucked some of the warmth out of the room. She abused the air further by pulling the moisture out of it. She formed a shield of water just in front of the flaming darts.

The fire crashed into the water, making a cloud of hissing steam.

The dragon hovered over Lorenzo, wings spread wide. Anise thought she saw a tiny glimpse of hazy gray sky through the small tear in one wing. Then she folded them together and dove down on the wizard. Anise marveled again at how a creature of such size could move with so much speed. The scene reminded her of a hawk diving down on a rabbit in an open field.

Lorenzo made a last effort and conjured another gust of wind toward the dragon. Still, with no time to prepare and the creature's momentum, it made no difference. There was a mighty crash as the dragon hit the mage and the floor. The hall shook yet again. Anise wasn't sure how anything could have survived that impact. But Lorenzo was still struggling weakly when the dragon launched herself into the air once again, with him clutched in her claws.

Flambé flew to a height just above the top of the walls and shook her prey like a cat shaking a captured mouse. Then she flung the wizard over the edge into the mists outside.

THE SCRYING POOL

1

A hush fell over the hall. The bubbling, fuming sound from the pool could be heard in the quiet. The dragon flapped her mighty wings and landed in the spot she had risen from. She looked around herself as if to say, "Who's next."

Anise looked over and saw, with great relief, that Briac was helping Sebastian to sit up. There were gleams of silvery-gray metal showing through the rents in his thistledown jerkin.

"My uncle wasn't trying to attack you," she snapped at the dragon, "he was coming to help."

Anise heard the dragon's voice in her head again. *If that's so, I'm sorry,* she thought. *You all look the same to me. Anyway, I regret biting him; he tasted terrible. Dragonsbane and spiders.* Flambé coughed and spat again.

The bubbling, fuming, and spurting noises from the stone pool behind Anise grew louder. It felt like the contents of the basin were about to erupt. Somehow, Anise had thought that the problem would be taken care of with Lorenzo gone. Now she realized that he had merely started something that wasn't just going to end with his absence. Somehow the pool would have to be closed, and the cracks in the barrier between reality and dream would need to be repaired.

"I'm here to help as well," she said. She gestured toward the seething pool. "Can you do something to stop this? Can you do something to stop the dream storms?"

A burst of greenish fluid exploded out of the basin. Anise avoided looking at the liquid as best she could. She felt its power pulling on her mind.

Can I? thought the dragon. *Can I? My kind doesn't do such things. We leave such forces alone: we know better. It took your kind to open these cracks; it is on you to close them.*

Briac and Sebastian, with Sebastian leaning heavily on Briac's shoulder, walked over to them. Anise noticed again the gleam of silvery-gray metal shining through the rents in Sebastian's jerkin. Flambé backed away from the tufts of thistledown falling from it.

Anise pulled her battered uncle into a long silent embrace. Her eyes filled with tears.

2

Another spurt of the green dream stuff exploded out of the pool. The bubbling seemed to be increasing with every minute. Flambé looked impatiently at Anise. She tilted her head to one side, and Anise heard her thoughts again.

There is another dream storm coming, she thought, *even stronger this time. You'd better hurry.*

"What am I supposed to do?" asked Anise.

I told you, thought the dragon, *I don't know. But, you had better do it fast.* She stepped back as if to watch what would happen next.

"Briac," called Anise, "Come help me." She ran over to the pool's edge and started trying to lift the iron lid. It was hinged on one side. The opposite end from the hinge had a solid-looking open padlock.

Briac started trying to lift the other side of the lid. Sebastian came over, walking gingerly, and tried his best to help.

"Don't look into the liquid," said Anise, "It's dangerous."

They managed to get the lid upright between the three of them, but when they tried to swing it over the spurting fluid, the cover bounced back from the dream stuff like it was repelled. In fact, each time the heavy metal lid came close to being in contact with the fluid, it was forced back so fiercely as to make trying to hold it dangerous.

Anise abandoned the attempt before anyone got hurt.

"I don't know what to do," she said sadly, looking at Briac and her uncle.

There was the sound of flapping wings, and a black raven emerged from the mists above the hall's walls. It flew a curving path around the bubbling fountain and landed on the green stone floor at Anise's feet.

     "Anise," said the bird quietly as it cocked its head to one side.

3

The black bird hopped forward on its claws, three little hops until it stood just in front of Anise. It was hard not to think of it as a bird, even though she knew it to be the lord of Dreams. "Lord Morpheus," she said, "can you help me with that?" She pointed to the spurting column of dream stuff.

"Anise," cawed the bird, "you don't need my help. You're a channeler in Dream. You do what you do best." Then the bird tilted its head to one side and continued, "Though I guess that's what channelers do best; they ask for help."

Anise pointed at the top of the wall. "What's going to happen to Lorenzo?" she asked.

The bird made a sound almost like a laugh. "He's fallen into the true dreaming beyond the Keep, not this half-dream we're in here," it cackled. "If he survives Lyssa, I'll make sure he's lost there for at least as long as you were."

Anise turned from the bird and walked over near the spouting basin. She avoided looking into the green geyser of fluid, sat cross-legged on the floor, and closed her eyes. As in the mists outside the keep, she tried to reach out with that part of her mind that she used when she called up a channeling dream.

Trying to channel without sleeping felt odd. Except for calling Morpheus, she hadn't attempted it since before her time at the Academy. Still, she drew on her recollection of her games with Sebastian and Isabel's chickens and her encounter with the wolves when she first traveled to the Academy. Soon enough, she felt herself drifting into a welcome daydream. The sensation of power that flooded into her made her feel strong.

4

The familiar feeling of being in her circle of light in a channeling dream flooded Anise. Without opening her eyes or rising, she found herself standing with her eyes open in a room that she immediately recognized as Hades' throne room. On its raised dais at the far end of the room was Hades' ebony throne.

She walked toward the throne. Before she got halfway there, she was charged into by a furry thunderbolt of legs, heads, and licking tongues. When Cerberus put her paws up on Anise's black armored chest, the weight was enough to knock her backward. All three of the dog's heads were licking her face simultaneously.

"Cerberus," called out Hades. "Down, girl!" One of the heads pulled away from licking Anise and turned toward her master. "Down," the lord of the underworld called out again. The second pulled its tongue back from Anise's face. Lord Hades scowled at the last head and said, "And you!" Cerberus stopped licking Anise and crept back to her master's side sheepishly. All three of her faces were looking at the ground, and her serpent-like tail was between her legs. Hades turned to Anise and said, "Anise, it's good you're here. We don't have much time."

Cerberus pushed up against her master's side. She lifted all three heads and gazed at Anise. Her center head's tongue was lolling out and drooling slightly. The leftmost one panted.

"The doors are ready to open," said the lord of the dead. "Let's go back to the Keep."

"We can't go to the Keep," said Anise, "This is a channeling dream."

"Well, the Keep is in Dream," said Lord Hades. "Or, half in Dream, anyway. All you have to do is open your eyes. We'll meet the others there."

"The others?" asked Anise.

"Open your eyes, Anise," the lord of the underworld insisted.

5

Anise opened her eyes to the bubbling seething Scrying Pool. The fluid was fuming even more fiercely than before. The sensation of opening her eyes when she felt like they were already open was odd. She looked away from the pool so as not to be drawn in by the dream stuff. Briac and Sebastian were standing over her, looking worried.

Anise felt comforted by their concern for a moment, then the situation's urgency hit her, and she stood up.

The Hall of Doors looked the same as when she closed her eyes. The raven that was the Lord of Dream stood on the green floor, his beady black eyes fixed on her.

As she turned her gaze toward the bird, something started to change. The raven started getting bigger, growing upward, almost as fast as the spurting dream stuff in the Scrying Pool. The black feathers of its wings spread and widened until they turned into a black cloak on a tall, pale man. Lord Morpheus stood there, thin and smiling, looking just as he had when Anise first fell into Dream.

The Lord of Dream nodded to Anise and might have said something if he hadn't been cut short by one of the nearby doors opening.

It was a silver door, an inlay of a full moon in mother of pearl on its face. The woman who stepped out was dressed in a flowing gown. Both she and her gown glowed with the cool warmth of the full moon on a clear night.

"Mistress Luna," said Anise. She curtsied, only realizing when she reached down for a skirt that wasn't there that the black armor she had on didn't lend itself to the gesture.

"Anise," said the goddess of the moon, "It's good to see you again." Anise felt a flood of reassurance and calm filling her as she looked at the moon's beautiful face.

Luna turned to Sebastian. She smiled at him, then frowned slightly as she saw his state. The rents in his jerkin and his shredded white leggings made him look like he'd been ground under a millstone. Still, he stood straight and proud and returned her smile. She reached out and smoothed a disheveled lock of hair on his brow.

"And, who is this?" said the lunar goddess, looking at Briac. Briac didn't respond. He seemed mesmerized by the moon's cool glow.

They were interrupted by a blast of hot white light as another door opened.

6

I t was a golden door this time. On the surface, etched into the gold, was an image of a chariot pulled by two blazing horses. The god of the sun stepped out through the door frame. "Helios," called out Anise joyfully. Then she blushed, the bright light coming from the sun god's face and crown clearly showing her face's crimson flush, bowed, and said, "It's good to see you, Lord Helios."

The sun good looked as youthful and handsome as ever. His face shone with a bright smile as if he was about to burst out laughing. He looked around the room like it was the first time he saw it, walked over to where Anise and Luna were standing, and said, "Anise." He turned to Luna and continued, "Sister." Finally, the sun god turned his eye on Morpheus. His smile dimmed a little as he said, "Cousin." It seemed that was enough greeting for the sun god. He ignored Sebastian and Briac standing off to the side, and even Flambé. His gaze went beyond the black-robed Lord of Dream to take in the spurting fountain of dream stuff. "I guess we've got our work cut out for us," he said.

Another door opened. This one was black, with the image of a skull on it. Anise was hardly surprised to see Lord Hades, the lord of the underworld, step out to join the assembled group.

Sebastian and Briac were standing to one side, their mouths hanging open. Even if you didn't recognize them, the gods radiated a sense of power and presence. It made it hard to do anything other than standing still, gazing at them in awe.

There was a loud rapping noise. Anise looked around to see where it was coming from. It repeated. It came from a plain unmarked trapdoor in the green stone floor.

When no one else responded, Anise walked over to the

door. She opened it. A voice called out from below. "A little help, if you please."

Looking down, Anise saw a hand reaching upward, above a head of short curly brown hair. It was Koalemos. Anise reached down her hand and helped him clamber awkwardly up through the trapdoor. He puffed and panted a little as he collapsed on the green stone floor.

"Just let me catch my breath," he said. "That was a long climb."

7

After Koalemos caught his breath and rose to his feet, Hades spoke. "Well," he said, leaning his weight slightly on his bident scepter, "Now that we're all here, we'd better get started." Another surge of green fluid bubbled forth from the Scrying Pool behind him as if to frame his words.

Anise noticed, with some regret, that Cerberus hadn't accompanied her master on this outing. She took stock of the assembled collection of gods and wondered if this could really be her doing. She was somewhat accustomed to speaking to a single god or goddess in a channeling dream. Still, even just one was always an awe-inspiring experience. Five gods were standing around her. She felt like an ant looking up at a mountain.

Koalemos seemed to notice her disquiet. "We needed a powerful channeler to clean up someone's mess," he said. He glanced at Morpheus. Anise thought she saw Koalemos wink at the dream lord before turning his gaze to the ground.

Morpheus turned beet red for an instant. The flush was gone so quickly that it would have been hard to notice if it hadn't stood out so clearly on his pale face. The dream lord stood up a little straighter. "Well," he said, somewhat peevishly, "We can't all be as perfect as you, Koalemos."

Koalemos muttered under his breath, "Cole."

"We needed?" Anise asked.

"Huh?" said Koalemos.

"You said, 'We needed a powerful channeler,'" said Anise. "What did you mean by that?"

Koalemos smacked the palm of his hand against his forehead. "I've said too much," he said.

Hades interjected. "Enough of this. We have an important job to do and not that much time to do it in." He swept an arm across the pool behind himself. The seething and fuming hadn't calmed or slowed.

Flambé watched the proceedings with a difficult-to-read expression from the other side of the hall. Her expression might have shown skepticism, it might have shown hope, or it might have just been the inscrutability of her dragon face.

Hades met Anise's eyes and said, "Anise, if you're ready, I think you can begin."

8

A surge of panic filled Anise. "I can begin?" she practically shouted. "I have no idea what to do to stop this. You're the gods; you need to fix it." Hades looked taken aback. It wasn't clear anyone had ever spoken to him like that.

Luna stepped forward. She glowed with the quiet beauty of a full moon shining down on a flowing river at night. The peaceful smile on her face was immediately a balm to Anise's nerves. "Anise, dear," she said. "We're here to help you. There are rules. Sometimes the gods can't do things that mortals can." She reached out and put her hand gently on Anise's shoulder.

Anise felt a rush of cool calm flooding her body. Through Luna's touch on her shoulder, serenity, patience, and peace of mind flowed into her. *It's all right*, she thought, *it'll all be all right.* She looked around at the group. *Why does everyone look so nervous? We probably don't even have to do anything; the cracks will most likely close by themselves.*

Helios stepped closer to Anise. He reached out to put his hand on her shoulder next to his sister's. "Anise," he said, "Like Luna says, we're here to help you, but we need to act, and we need to act now."

Anise felt her confidence increase. He was right. She needed to take matters into her own hands. It was clear that the gods were not able to act. She had to be the one to make the changes that needed to be made. Action had to be taken and taken now. She started preparing her elemental abilities. *Perhaps I should start by blasting the dream stuff with ice?*

Hades looked nervous, seeing Anise beginning her preparations. It was the first time Anise had ever seen his demeanor crack. She wondered if it was the first time anyone had. He moved quickly over to her and put his hand on the other shoulder from the one the siblings were touching. "Anise," he said, "Let's not rush into anything before we're ready."

Anise felt a sense of control filling her. *Action*, she thought, *but calm, measured action. I will carefully decide what to do, then do it expediently, calmly, and with careful consideration.*

9

Anise felt in control. She felt calm, collected, and ready to act, but she still didn't know what to do. She looked at the assemblage of gods. Koalemos met her gaze. He reached out his hand and placed it next to Hades' on her shoulder.

A surge of something else filled Anise. She felt jubilant, wild, reckless. She felt powerful. Anise, the person, faded into the background. Anise, the goddess, looked around the room with new eyes.

"Now, Anise," said Koalemos.

Anise reached out toward the metal cover of the Scrying Pool. Briac and Sebastian lifted it again to a vertical position. She could feel the surging dream stuff on the other side of the metal as she touched the lid.

Everything became very clear to Anise, the goddess. The dream stuff was just an element like Air, Fire, Water, or Earth; she could manipulate it in the same way. The bubbling, seething pool on the other side of the lid still made it impossible for Briac and Sebastian to close the cover. Anise reached out with her mind to pull some reality and truth from the air and use it to calm the turbulent dream fluid.

The fuming geyser of green dream stuff started subsiding. Briac and Sebastian lowered the lid as the bubbling lessened. When the cover dropped onto the stone of the pool edge, Briac ran over and snapped the padlock closed.

Anise stood, her hand still on the lid of the Scrying Pool, the four gods' hands still on her shoulders. She wasn't done. Not even close. She could feel the dream stuff under the lid, still seething and searching for a way to pop free. She could also feel the cracks extending out from here, from the pool, the center of the web. She could see the invisible tendrils of weakness extending from the basin, the hub, out to each of the doors in the room where they began their paths.

10

She closed her eyes. She would have to use other senses for this next part. The floods of calm, energy, control, and exhilaration from the gods' hands on her shoulders continued. Anise, the goddess, started to wonder if there was any reason she should have to go back to just being Anise, the person.

The spiders' web of broken cracks radiating outward from the central hub of the Scrying Pool surrounded her. Some were thicker and more established; some were narrow paths that only a few clairvoyants had walked. Anise could feel the cracks, and she could feel how they were weakening the structure of the veil between Dream and the waking world.

She felt along the paths. Clairvoyants walked them even now. She sensed each consciousness as a bubble on the crack it traveled. She could also sense how each clairvoyant was deepening and widening the path they walked.

She laughed. The feeling of power increased. With a surge of her manipulation of the element of dream stuff, she popped the traveling clairvoyants off their journeys and back to the waking world.

Anise, the person, had a moment of clarity. *They've trained for years to be clairvoyants. When I'm done, their livelihood will be gone.*

Anise, the goddess, didn't share her concern. *Let them read tea leaves or tarot cards; who cares.*

Anise's spirit hovered over the realm of Dream. The spiderweb of cracks, now empty of travelers, surrounded her. With her distant body back in the keep imitating her mind's gesture, Anise reached out her hand and pinched the first crack shut. She squeezed her fingers together, compressing the split between the realm of Dream and the waking world, and slid her paired fingers along the crack. There was an enormous feeling of satisfaction as the two sides of the slit merged, and the damage disappeared.

Back in the keep, Briac and Sebastian watched as the doors of the Hall of Doors disappeared one at a time.

11

The fluid under the cover in the scrying pool was calm and settled like still water on a lake. Anise opened her eyes to a hall that would have to be renamed. Except for the open double doors at the end of the hall, all the other doors were gone. She still felt the power surging into her from the gods' hands on her shoulders.

She looked around herself eagerly. *What should she fix next?* She could take care of the Grisput problem. She could make sure Lorenzo never returned from the realm of Dream to hurt anyone ever again. She could push the Keep further into the dreaming realm so that no one from the waking world ever stumbled across it.

Anise lifted her hands to make a gesture of power. It occurred to her that she didn't need to do such mundane things as make a hand gesture anymore. With the power surging into her, she could do almost anything with a thought, but old habits die hard.

She started. There was a drop in her power, a reduction in her godliness. Luna had lifted her hand from Anise's shoulder. The calm and peace that she had been providing Anise were gone.

Anise was filled with rage. *How dare they!* With a flip of her wrist, she changed her perspective, and suddenly, she was looking down on the three little godlets that still had their hands on her shoulders. They were nothing. They were ants looking up at the glory of Anise, the goddess!

Anise prepared to blast the tiny things. They had no worth. Hades with his little underworld, Helios with his connection to the sun, Koalemos with whatever he was. They were little provincial powerless beings. She was the goddess of everything.

Helios removed his hand from her shoulder. Anise reconsidered. She would still take her revenge on these little things for trying to take away her power. She would do it methodically, with careful consideration.

Hades removed his hand. Anise started laughing. She had less power, it was true, but she had freedom. She could do with it what she willed.

Koalemos lifted his hand from Anise's shoulder. She blinked, then turned her head toward Briac and Sebastian standing nearby.

Anise took a step toward Sebastian, lifted her hand in his direction, said, "Uncle," and started to collapse as if her legs no longer had any strength. Sebastian caught her before her body hit the smooth stone floor, his eyes filled with concern.

Raphael charged into the hall through the open double doors at the end of the room. He held his gleaming sword. Iggy hissed confrontationally on his shoulder.

"Where's Lorenzo," he shouted.

EPILOGUE

When Anise had recovered enough to make the trip, she and Sebastian traveled to Capitol. They met with king Twilight and convinced him that he was, in fact, Sebastian's son. Their subsequent journey to Hero and Isabel's tears and jubilation are tales for another time.

Twilight discovered he had a family he had never known, including a younger sister, Sunshine, who he'd never met. He offered to introduce her to the court, but Sebastian and Isabel were convinced that she wasn't ready for that yet.

The masters at the Academy recognized that clairvoyance should no longer be taught at the school. They accepted this partly due to reported events but mostly because clairvoyance simply didn't work anymore. The clairvoyants who'd hung up a shingle with an eye symbol had to close up shop. They found that they could no longer travel the paths of truth, and they also couldn't even find their way to the Room of Doors.

Rafael became a famous hero, with Iggy by his side. He left Ashton to explore the roads and by-ways of Liamec. They became known for their ability to resolve supernatural conflicts civilly.

The realization that the girl of his dreams didn't dream of him as he dreamed of her released Rafael from a common fate as a villager. That moment inspired him to leave Ashton and go out and become the hero he was to become.

Raphael's sword eventually spoke to him. The first thing she said was, "You're not Ed. Where's Ed?"

One of Rafael and Iggy's adventures was a trip to the elemental plane of Fire. Iggy's family was happy to welcome the prodigal flame home.

Briac wrote a ballad called "God Touched." It became one of the most popular songs of the next few hundred years, enhancing Anise and Briac's reputations. It's entirely possible that having written such a popular ballad helped confirm Briac's ascension to the rank of master bard, but who knows for sure.

But these are tales for another time.

J. STEVEN LAMPERTI

Dear Reader,

Thank you for reading *Death & Dragon*. I hope the fates of Anise and those who walked beside her have stayed with you, as they have with me.

If this trilogy was your first visit to Liamec, you may be glad to know that its stories continue in the *Tales of Liamec* series. And if you arrived here from those tales, I hope this volume has deepened your sense of the world and the threads that bind it together.

For those curious about what became of Twilight—Sebastian and Isabel's lost son—*The Wolf's Tooth* offers a glimpse into his early years. And if you've grown fond of Rafael, Iggy, and Sunshine, their adventures continue in *Sunshine Over Hero*, a tale of monsters, misunderstandings, and a sword with far too many opinions.

If this trilogy's conclusion brought you joy, I'd be truly grateful if you shared a quick review on Amazon. Your words help other readers find these stories—and help me keep writing them.

With thanks and wonder,
J. Steven Lamperti

ACKNOWLEDGEMENT

Thanks to my beta readers: Claudia, John, Page, Mary, Harris, and Joerg. Also, as always, to my alpha, Andrea.

BOOKS IN THIS SERIES

The Channeler Trilogy

Moon & Shadow

A young man takes the moon from the sky. The village wants to know why.

Sebastian isn't sure what possessed him. One quiet evening, he reached up, took the moon from the sky, and hung it above his hearth. Since then, strange things have followed—things he calls gifts, though no one offered them: the shadows of his true love's feet, the breath of a dreaming dog, a sword that remembers war.

Magic has taken an interest in Sebastian. But it isn't his doing—and it isn't done with him yet.

As his quiet village stirs with wonder, suspicion, and something darker, Sebastian is drawn into a story far bigger than himself—one that begins with a mysterious girl named Anise and won't end until the world remembers how it dreams.

Wry, whimsical, and full of quiet marvels, Moon & Shadow is the first book in the Channeler Trilogy. Perfect for readers who love Diana Wynne Jones and The Girl Who Drank the Moon.

Sun & Dream

Dreams can change the world—if they don't change her first.

Anise has always lived half in dreams. But when she begins her training at the Academy—a hidden school where magic and dreams entwine—her quiet life in the village of Hero fades into memory.

There, among scholars, mages, and strange gods, Anise discovers that her gift for channeling daemons is far greater—and far more dangerous—than she ever imagined.

Whispers swirl through the Academy's halls. Secrets glimmer behind friendly faces. And somewhere between sunlit classrooms and shadowed dreams, Anise must decide who she can trust—including a golden-eyed god who speaks of destiny.

In a world where dreams shape reality, mastering her magic may be the only way to save everything she loves.

BOOKS BY THIS AUTHOR

The Wolf's Tooth

Raised by wolves. Hunted for a secret he doesn't understand.

Twee never chose the wild, but it raised him all the same. After fire scatters his pack, he's swept into a world of outlaws, city streets, and forge smoke. In Grisput, a city that sells its servants and forgets its poor, he learns to work iron—and meets a red-haired street girl with magic in her pockets and more to her past than she lets on.

But whispers of a clairvoyant's prophecy follow him, and the King's Guard has begun to listen.

For readers who love A Wizard of Earthsea and Stardust, The Wolf's Tooth is a warm, wondrous coming-of-age tale about finding kinship in unexpected places—and strength in the quiet heart of a boy who never asked to be special.

Step into the forest. Follow the smoke. The story begins where the wild things run.

Perfect for readers who love quiet heroes, slow-burn wonder, and fantasy that grows from the roots up.

By The Sea

The sea took her brother. Now, it's calling her name.

Years after a storm claimed her brother's life, Annabelle Fisher still walks the shoreline—but she keeps her heart turned away from the sea, and from anyone whose eyes dance with the waves.

When a handsome stranger delivers a formal invitation to a ball at the duke's castle, her carefully quiet life begins to unravel. What begins with a single dance draws her into a world of ancient rivalries and ocean-born secrets.

Beneath the surface lies a mythic realm ruled by gods, where memories twist like currents and love can't be trusted. To protect the family she has left, Annabelle must follow a path that leads through longing, grief—and into the shadowed halls of Hades himself.

Lyrical and sea-swept, By the Sea is a romantic YA fantasy of loss, courage, and ocean magic—perfect for fans of The Scorpio Races and The Girl Who Fell Beneath the Sea.

Twilight's Fall

A quiet guardsman. A fallen king. A kingdom on the edge of ruin.

Corentin never wanted to be a hero. But when an ambush shatters King Twilight's journey home from the far reaches of his realm, he finds himself on the run with the young monarch —and two unexpected allies: Aela, an herbalist with sharp eyes and a steadier heart, and Blaine, a fellow guardsman who escaped the ambush at his side.

As old loyalties crumble and secrets rise from the shadows, Corentin must reckon with a legacy he never asked for—and a power buried deeper than he knows. To protect the king, he'll have to step out of the quiet and into the fight for Liamec's future.

Blending myth, tenderness, and slow-burning romance, Twilight's Fall is a richly woven YA fantasy for fans of The Queen of the Tearling and The Bone Houses.

Sunshine Over Hero

Strange things are happening in the village of Hero.

First it was the sheep—found drained of blood. Then village girls began to disappear, returning days later with no memory of where they'd been.

Sunny, a sharp-minded farm girl with no patience for nonsense, is sure something unnatural is behind it. But when Raphael shows up—a traveling monster hunter whose last case involved a mouse spirit stealing cheese—she realizes help might not be as heroic as she'd hoped.

Raphael does have a few advantages: a talking silver sword named Cutter, a fire imp named Iggy who only ever says "Burn," and a willingness to follow Sunny's lead. The only problem? Cutter's eloquence and Iggy's enthusiasm don't always mix.

As the mystery deepens, Sunny and Raphael uncover an ancient threat—and an unexpected connection that neither of them saw coming.

The Pirates Of Meara

A silver-eyed girl washes up from the sea, and nothing in Mouse's life is quiet again.

Fern is a duke's daughter, stolen by pirates and cast ashore in a city she doesn't understand.

Mouse is a street orphan who thought he knew Meara—until the city begins whispering secrets only he can hear.

Now the pirate Bluebeard hunts them both. Fern thinks it's for ransom. But the truth runs deeper, hidden in stone and salt.

Because Mouse isn't just a quiet boy with a borrowed name —he's the key to an undersea world, and the city has not forgotten.

The Pirates of Meara is a gentle, magical tale of friendship, lost cities, and the tide that pulls us home—perfect for fans of The Chronicles of Prydain and The True Confessions of Charlotte Doyle.

For readers who love quiet heroes, sea-swept wonder, and cities where the past still stirs.

Endymion And The Fae

Endymion is a shepherd of the high pastures, where the wind carries old songs and the sheep know every stone.

His life is simple—until he meets Lily, a fae girl with wild eyes and a laugh like spring water.

Their bond is gentle at first, yet the world around them is not. Villagers whisper that the fae bring trouble. The Wee Folk say humans cannot be trusted. Suspicion grows, and tender love carries a cost.

When old tensions rise again, Endymion must choose between peace and passion, tradition and hope. If he and Lily cannot bridge the divide, both may lose more than their hearts.

Though part of the Tales of Liamec, Endymion and Lily's tale can be read alone—a song of its own beneath the wide sky.

Told with the lilt of folklore and the hush of mountain vales, Endymion and the Fae is a pastoral romantic fantasy of first love, quiet rebellion, and the fragile magic that binds two hearts and two worlds—for readers who love gentle fantasy, slow-burn romance, and the stillness of high pastures.